NEIL ARMSTRONG IS MY UNCLE

& OTHER LIES MUSCLE MAN McGINTY TOLD ME

Nan Marino

SCHOLASTIC INC.
New York Toronto London Auckland
Sydney Mexico City New Delhi Hong Kong

ISBN 978-0-545-23997-4

Text copyright © 2009 by Nan Marino. All rights reserved.
Published by Scholastic Inc., 557 Broadway, New York, NY 10012,
by arrangement with Roaring Brook Press, a division of Holtzbrinck
Publishing Holdings Limited Partnership. SCHOLASTIC and
associated logos are trademarks and/or registered trademarks
of Scholastic Inc.

12 11 10 9 8 7 6 5 4 3 2   10 11 12 13 14 15/0

Printed in the U.S.A.   40

First Scholastic printing, January 2010

Book design by Kimi Weart

To my husband, Sal
and
to my real-life Kebsie Grobsers

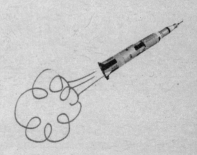

CHAPTER ONE

The Blizzard of '69

MUSCLE MAN MCGINTY is a squirrelly runt, a lying snake, and a pitiful excuse for a ten-year-old. The problem is that no one on Ramble Street knows it but me. In the entire town of Massapequa Park, only I see him for what he really is. A phony.

Knowing the truth when others fail to see it is hard on a person. That's because the truth has a way of seeping under your skin and wrapping itself around you, like a coiled-up Slinky.

You know that tinny sound a Slinky makes? *Shink. Shink. Shink.*

Sometimes I hear it creeping around inside my brain.

The closer I get to Muscle Man, the louder it gets. When he's standing right next to me spewing out his whoppers, that Slinky inside me goes crazy.

SHINK! SHINK! SHINK! You can only imagine my headaches. I've even named the really big ones "Muscle Men" after the cause of all my problems.

Personally, I think it's funny to name your pain, but the others on Ramble Street never get my humor. Even Big Danny, who can laugh at dead teacher jokes, fails to see the comedy.

"Jeez, Tamara," he huffs. "The kid only moved here a few weeks ago. Can't you give him a break?" He kicks his foot at the side of the curb.

"Jeez yourself," is all I think of saying back.

Big Danny turns his back on me, and I turn my back on him. We are both standing at the corner of Ramble Street, each one staring in the opposite direction. Neither one of us will give up our spot on the sidewalk because the ice cream truck is about to come around for the first time this season.

It is an important day. Ice cream trucks mean summer is here. No more having Mrs. Webber, my fifth grade teacher, glaring at me through her spectacles. As far as I'm concerned, ice-cream trucks never come soon enough, and they leave far too early. Their time on Ramble Street is fleeting. And if Big Danny wants to ruin the entire morning by not speaking, that's fine with me. It'll be easier to hear the bells without his blabbering.

We wait in stony silence. Every once in a while, I flip my ponytail in his direction just to annoy him.

It's not until Muscle Man McGinty pulls up on his bicycle that Big Danny starts yapping. All that time, Big Danny had something he was itching to tell. As soon as he sees Muscle Man, he blurts it out.

"I made the swim team!" shouts Big Danny.

"Hey, good for you, Big Guy!" Muscle Man pats him on the back. "Making the swim team is not an easy thing to do."

"Yeah, congratulations," I mumble, not sure if Big Danny is talking to me yet.

"I heard there was a lot of competition," says Muscle Man.

Big Danny grins.

Muscle Man is wormy. He always starts with something nice before he slides into one of his whoppers.

I hold my breath, waiting for what comes next.

"Did I happen to mention I'm training for the Olympics in that same sport?" Muscle Man says.

Sure. And I'm waiting for Captain Kirk to beam me up to the starship *Enterprise*.

"Every Sunday, Wednesday, and Friday morning, I go to the pool and practice." He puffs out his puny chest.

"My coach thinks I'll win a gold medal in seven races. It would be a world record, but I'm hopeful."

"You like to swim?" asks Big Danny, like it's every day someone announces he's training for the Olympics.

"Yep. Coach says I'll be ready for Munich, Germany. That's where the next games will be." Muscle Man presses his thumb and forefinger so close together they almost touch. "I'm this far away from the world record. All I need to do is work on my flip turn."

Turn, schmurn. First of all, Muscle Man is barely ten, which means that in 1972, when they have the next Olympics, he'll only be about thirteen. Plus, I've never seen him swim. I doubt the kid even owns a bathing suit. World record, my eye. This kid's got as much chance of going to Munich, Germany, as I have of going to the moon.

"Maybe we could go to the pool together," Big Danny says.

"Yeah, and you can both practice for that world's record," I say, with disbelief dripping off my every word.

Big Danny catches my tone and sneers at me. At me! Muscle Man sells him a bag of bull and gets nothing, and I get glared at for pointing out the obvious.

I turn away from both of them, pretending to be interested in a group of ants climbing over a half-eaten Tootsie Roll. Neither boy notices. They're too busy talking about backstrokes and racing dives.

"Of course, no matter how famous I become, I'll always remember my friends on Ramble Street," says Muscle Man.

The spot above my right temple begins to throb.

Muscle Man puts his arm on Big Danny's shoulder. "I'll never forget you, Danny O. And you too, Tamara."

I refuse to even look his way. Instead, I watch a tiny dandelion seed float on the breeze. I catch it before it finds its way to the ground.

"They'll probably want to put my picture on the Wheaties box," he says.

"Jeez. Give me a break." I throw my hands up in the air. Before I can tell him what I think of his lies, I catch another dandelion seed. Soon, my hands are full of them. A flurry of white surrounds us.

Muscle Man looks around. "Where's it coming from?"

Big Danny points to my house. "Tammy's mom."

I glance across the street to where Shirley is wrestling with the dandelions that fill our front lawn. With every pull, she sends up another flurry.

"There must be hundreds of them," says Big Danny.

"Millions," says Muscle Man, which is another lie. I highly doubt there are a million. A hundred thousand, maybe, but not a million.

Shirley yanks harder, and the flurry turns into a blizzard. Like snowflakes, the seeds twist and tumble before they find their way onto the lawns of Ramble Street.

"Cool." Muscle Man cups his hand to catch a seed. Then he jabs at me playfully. "Hey, Tammy. Listen."

I'm about to tell him that he's got nothing to say that I want to listen to when I realize what he's talking about.

Bells ring out in the distance. The Mr. Softee song grows louder.

Any second now that truck will turn the corner. Right in the middle of the dandelion blizzard, summer will come to Ramble Street.

CHAPTER TWO

Just Plain Wrong

"THE ICE CREAM MAN is coming!" Big Danny and Muscle Man call out to the other kids on the block.

"You don't have to scream that loud," I whisper, pushing away the dandelion seeds that circle round us.

"We have to tell the others. We do it every year," says Big Danny, and he shouts again.

"Can't we do it a different way? One that is less noisy?" I worry that their racket will alert my mother. So far, she hasn't noticed me. But if she looks up, my lazy summer day is over. Shirley is not a person who faces dandelions alone.

I shift back and forth between Big Danny and Muscle Man, trying my best to look invisible. Benny Schuster, who's a head taller than any kid in our grade, pulls up on his bike. I slip behind him, ducking out of site of Shirley and her weeds.

Mr. Grabowsky hurries toward us. MaryBeth and her little sister, Janie Lee, skip circles round him. Before they step onto the street, Mr. Grabowsky grabs onto each girl's hand, holding them tight, like they're precious butterflies about to fly away. But trust me, there is nothing precious about MaryBeth Grabowsky.

We nod hello. Muscle Man points to the baseball cap Mr. Grabowsky wears every Saturday. "How about those Mets? Think they'll win today?"

Mr. Grabowsky is too busy watching the latest flurry of dandelion puffs to answer. He glances nervously at his front lawn, where perfect blades of grass stand like soldiers in formation.

Muscle Man shows them his hand filled with seeds. "Isn't it cool? Like snow on Christmas morning!"

All three Grabowskys throw me the exact same look at once, and I doubt that even five-year-old Janie Lee thinks there's anything cool about dandelion seeds. I don't know what they're all so worried about. No self-respecting weed would dare grow on the Grabowsky front lawn.

"Mr. Softee's here! I see it!" shouts Big Danny.

"It's turning down Ramble Street!" says Muscle Man.

"Finally," says Benny Schuster.

I run my fingers over the quarter and two dimes in my back pocket, grateful that my father remembered to give me my allowance and that I've got enough money for extra sprinkles. My mouth begins to water.

We form a line. Big Danny is first, then Benny Schuster, with me hiding behind him. The Grabowsky girls are next. John Marcos pulls up on his brand-new Sting-Ray. Big Danny, Benny Schuster, and I eye John's new bike while MaryBeth Grabowsky eyes John Marcos.

Muscle Man turns to leave.

"Where are you going?" asks MaryBeth, who can never resist poking her nose into other people's business.

Muscle Man pats his belly. "I had a truckload of Mr. Softee yesterday. I just don't think I could eat any more today."

"The ice cream truck didn't come yesterday. That's impossible," I say. I look to the others to back me up, but no one says a word except for Mr. Grabowsky.

He flashes a dollar bill. "I wouldn't want to force you, son, but I was hoping you'd join me and the girls for a cone today."

Muscle Man beelines back to the Mr. Softee truck. "I suppose I'd have room for one more cone."

Mr. Grabowsky, who once told me that I was on a slippery slope for lying about denting his car with a baseball, seems perfectly fine with Muscle Man's made-up tale about the ice-cream truck. He musses Muscle Man's hair.

"Tamara!" Shirley's voice slices through the Mr. Softee chimes. "Come help me with these weeds!"

I pretend I don't hear her and order a vanilla cone with chocolate sprinkles.

"Your mother's calling," whispers Big Danny, and I pretend I don't hear him either.

John Marcos looks worried. "Tammy, you'd better go."

Mr. Grabowsky clears his throat, and MaryBeth lets out a long, obnoxious sigh.

I shrug like I don't care, but my shoulders feel heavy from the weight of all those stares.

"Ta-maaarh-rah!" Shirley is getting louder. "You know the rules about ice cream before lunch."

The ice-cream man hands me my cone, and I take my first lick.

Mr. Grabowsky gives me a look, and I wonder if I'm going to get the speech about being on a slippery slope. If my mouth wasn't so jammed with ice cream, I'd tell him that the lying runt standing next to his precious girls should hear his speech about sliding down the path to juvenile delinquency. After all, Muscle Man is the liar. All I'm doing is trying to eat my cone.

"Next," says the Mr. Softee man, but seven pairs of eyes are too busy watching me to answer.

I ignore them and do my best to stuff my face. The ice

cream is losing its taste, I'm wolfing it down so fast.

"Anyone want sprinkles?" asks Mr. Softee. "Anyone want some ice cream here?" And seven pairs of eyes turn back to the ice-cream man.

Mr. Grabowsky orders four double cones. One for him. One for each of his girls. And one for Muscle Man McGinty.

"If it wouldn't be too much trouble, I'd love some colored sprinkles, Mr. Grabowsky." Muscle Man tugs on Mr. Grabowsky's arm, and something cold does a backflip in my belly.

The simple act of eating an ice-cream cone gets me nothing but dirty looks, and what does Muscle Man get for telling his lies? Invitations to pools. Hair musses. Double cones with extra sprinkles.

I don't get it.

What Muscle Man does is wrong. Just plain wrong.

And everyone on Ramble Street knows it.

And they do nothing.

That's wrong too.

He needs to be stopped.

And I'm the one to do it.

With a flurry of seeds swirling around me, I make a solemn vow. I swear to the Slinky flopping around inside me that I will show the people of Ramble Street the real

Muscle Man McGinty. Somehow, some way, they will know what I know. I will not keep the truth locked inside me. I will set my Slinky free.

I shove the last bit of ice cream into my mouth and hurry across the street to Shirley and her dandelions.

CHAPTER THREE

Barbies Are
A Girl's Best Friend

A FEW DAYS later, I'm hardly out my front door when MaryBeth Grabowsky comes barreling toward me.

"Guess what?"

I don't even have time to shrug before she answers.

"I'm getting three more Barbies for my birthday. Know how many I'll have then?"

She doesn't wait for a reply.

"Thirteen." She waves a fist full of dolls in front of me. I can't help notice that they're all dressed in the same blue and green tennis dress, and that MaryBeth Grabowsky's tennis dress is a pretty good match too.

I march past her and head for the sidewalk, walking fast

like I have somewhere important to go. But before I can make an escape, MaryBeth races to my side.

"How many do you have, Tamara?" she asks in a voice sweeter than hot fudge.

This time, instead of spewing out the answer, she waits.

I give an empty 7Up can a good kick. It sails across the street and rolls sideways until it stops near the house where Kebsie Grobser used to live.

Kebsie is the kid I like better than all of the other kids on Ramble Street put together. I'll give you a hundred MaryBeth Grabowskys and all of their combined Barbie dolls for just one Kebsie Grobser.

A month and a half ago, Kebsie moved away, leaving me to face MaryBeth Grabowsky alone.

"How many Barbies did you say you have?" she asks again. This time her voice sounds like *double* fudge.

I chase after the 7Up can, but MaryBeth is right behind me, waiting for an answer. I take a deep breath and get it over with. "Two," I mumble.

Even though it's no big secret, something about having to say it out loud makes me feel lousy. In MaryBeth's eyes, no matter what I do in life, I'll always be a person worthy of only two Barbies, while she is worthy of thirteen.

Before she makes me feel any worse, I give the can another kick. It bangs into the front door of Kebsie's old house and ricochets off into the bushes.

The door opens.

"Nice kick, Tamara," says the most annoying voice in the world.

I stare down at the can—anything to avoid having to look at Muscle Man McGinty.

"When someone pays you a compliment, Tamara, you're supposed to say 'Thank you,'" says MaryBeth. "He just told you it was a nice kick."

I *knew* that. But I couldn't give Muscle Man the satisfaction of a thank you. He didn't deserve it, especially since he's been living in Kebsie Grobser's house for well over a month now.

For forty-two days, he's been going through Kebsie Grobser's front door and sitting on Kebsie Grobser's front steps. I bet he has her old bedroom. His view of Ramble Street from the top window belongs to Kebsie Grobser too.

Muscle Man jumps into the bushes.

"Here." He holds the can in front of me, but I'm not taking even as much as a piece of garbage from him.

I cross my arms, waiting for him to try to shove it at me.

Muscle Man grins. "I have something better than that for you. I've had it in my pocket for a week. But every time I see you, you're running off."

Not running off. Running away. That is more the truth. And I'd tell him that, too, except for the fact that MaryBeth Grabowsky would stick in her two cents.

Muscle Man reaches into his back pocket and pulls out a silver chain with a charm dangling from it. He tosses it to me.

Even before I catch it, I know what it is.

"I found it in my closet," Muscle Man says. "My grandma said that you'd want it."

I wrap my fist around the necklace so tight that it hurts my hand. But MaryBeth sees it anyway.

"Did that say *BF*?" she asks, and I wonder if she secretly took Miss Evelyn Wood's course in speed-reading.

I don't answer.

"Who is BF?" asks Muscle Man.

"It's not anyone's initials. It stands for 'Best Friend,'" says MaryBeth. "You only give it to someone very special."

"It's Kebsie's," I mumble.

MaryBeth turns to Muscle Man. "Kebsie Grobser lived here before you. She was a foster kid, like you. Mrs. Kutchner was her foster grandmother too."

"Oh." Muscle Man seems more interested in straightening out his shoelaces than in learning about Kebsie Grobser.

"Kebsie moved back with her mom," adds MaryBeth.

"She did?" I ask. "How do you know that?"

"*Everybody* knows that. My mom told me." She turns to Muscle Man. "I don't remember when Kebsie moved out *exactly*, but it was a few days before you moved in."

"Forty-two days ago," I tell her. At least I know that much. But that was all I knew.

Forty-two days ago, I came back from a four-day visit at Aunt Maria's and went to call for Kebsie, like I always did, and Mrs. Kutchner told me that she was gone.

"Well, aren't you glad that I found it on the bottom of my closet?" he asks.

"That was very nice of you," says MaryBeth.

"I happen to have superior vision," says Muscle Man. "Dr. Dan, my eye doctor, says he's never seen a human being who could see such a great distance. He said that I should be working as a top secret spy or something."

"Yeah, right. Maybe you'll be the next James Bond." I mean it as a joke, just like I mean the name Muscle Man as a joke. He's a pale, skinny kid with dirty hair and a runny nose. There's nothing muscley about him.

But Muscle Man doesn't get it, and as soon as I mention the name James Bond, he smiles.

For a second, no one speaks. MaryBeth and Muscle Man stare at me, as if they're waiting for something.

"What?" I say, finally.

MaryBeth puts her hands on her hips. "Well . . . he did find the charm. Don't you think *this* deserves a thank-you?"

Thanks? What does she want me to say thanks for? For

taking the room of my very best friend? For eating Kebsie Grobser's SpaghettiOs and drinking Kebsie Grobser's Hi-C? For creeping around a house that, as far as I'm concerned, belongs to Kebsie Grobser?

I hold back about a million tears, making sure that not a single one escapes and runs across my face. The last thing I want to do is cry in front of Muscle Man and MaryBeth Grabowsky.

My throat feels too lumpy to say anything anyway. I shove the BF charm into my pocket and race toward home.

CHAPTER FOUR

Full Moons, New Moons, Waning Gibbous

THAT NIGHT, I have an empty feeling in the pit of my stomach, one that no amount of Oreo cookies can make go away. I am positive about the cookies because as soon as Muscle Man threw me the BF charm, I ran home and ate an entire box.

The emptiness started the day I learned that Kebsie moved from Ramble Street. Nighttime makes it worse, and sleeping is near impossible. Instead of wrestling with my sheet and pillows, I stare out my bedroom window and think of Kebsie.

There's so much to wonder about. I wonder where she lives and if she has her Bobby Sherman poster on the wall and if she has new friends. Mostly I wonder if Kebsie is thinking of me, and if she has an empty feeling too.

I push open the window and climb outside to the roof of the garage. The warm air sticks to my skin. I wait for my eyes to get used to the dark and then find my way along the tar paper. When I reach the edge, I sit down and let my feet swing down toward Ramble Street.

In the entire town of Massapequa Park, there's no place like the garage rooftop. It's above the glare of the streetlights, so I get a clear view of the stars and the moon. When I look down, I can see every house on our block, from Old Mrs. Murphy's house crammed with flowers to Conchetta Marchetta's house crammed with kids.

But the best thing about the roof is that no one knows I'm here. I've been coming out since I was eight and haven't got caught yet.

In the forty-two days since Kebsie left, I've learned that there's only one thing that can help when I'm missing her.

A howl at the moon.

"Argooo!" My first try sounds like a squeaky sneeze.

Kebsie would be disappointed. She was the expert. Full moons. New moons. Crescent moons. Waxing gibbous. Waning gibbous. Quarter moons. Kebsie knew about every phase of the moon and howled at each and every one.

It drove the adults on Ramble Street crazy. You should hear the fuss they all made. MaryBeth Grabowsky said her parents complained about Kebsie every morning. Shirley said that all those TV shows about werewolves and vampires did a job on Kebsie's brain.

At first, I didn't know what to think. A howling girl is not exactly a common thing to find on Ramble Street. But Kebsie didn't care what anyone thought, even me. She was fearless. And I loved her for it.

I never howled when Kebsie was here. I was too afraid to try. She'd climb on top of Mrs. Kutchner's garage roof and make a racket, while I pressed myself flat against my own roof, trying my best to looking invisible, worried my parents would catch me. Nights like tonight, when the moon is full and bright, made me especially nervous.

I take a deep breath and give it another try.

"Argooooo!"

Better, but still not great.

I look across the street to Mrs. Kutchner's empty garage roof and try again.

"Arrooo!" My last one is almost perfect. I can see why this was Kebsie's joy.

I'm about to give it one more try when Marshall calls.

"Tamara! Is that you? Are you making that noise?" His voice is muffled so I can tell he's still in his bedroom.

I climb back through the window and slink under my covers. "No, Daddy."

I hear footsteps, quick ones, heading my way. They

stop at the foot of the stairs. "Do you have any idea how early I have to wake up?" Marshall yells, and I'm suddenly grateful that my parents are stair shouters and not face-to-face yellers like Big Danny's mom and dad. For now, my garage roof secret is safe.

"What are you doing up there?"

"Nothing, Daddy."

"Do you know what time my train comes in the morning?"

"7:11," I say, because he tells me all the time.

"Do you think it's easy having to take the Long Island Railroad into the city and then work eight long hours and then take the train all the way back to Massapequa Park every day?"

"No, Daddy."

"Are you trying to make my life difficult? Is that what you're doing up there?" he asks.

Every bone in my body wants to scream, "You betcha!" If Kebsie were here, that's what she'd say. No. If Kebsie were here, she'd say, "You betcha, *Marshall*," because Kebsie believes you shouldn't take any flack from anyone, and she calls everyone, even grown-ups, by their first names directly to their faces and not just behind their backs, like I do.

You should have seen Mrs. Webber's jaw drop the day Kebsie marched into the classroom and said, "Hi, Agnes."

Even my older brother Tim wouldn't have had the guts to do that, and he's in college.

"Tamara, I'm talking to you. Are you trying to make my life difficult?" my father asks again.

I think of Kebsie, and I mouth the words "You betcha, Marshall." But my out-loud words are, "No, Daddy."

"Then for Pete's sake, get to sleep!" His footsteps fade back toward his bedroom.

I grab the BF charm and tuck it under my pillow. I lie in my bed with my head where my feet should be so I can get a good look at the moon. And I wonder if Kebsie is howling, wherever she is.

CHAPTER FIVE

An In-Person Friend

THE NEXT MORNING, as soon as I see my face in the mirror, I notice it. The initials *BF* are indented into my cheek. Stupid pillow. It must have slid away from me in the middle of the night so there was nothing separating me from Kebsie's necklace.

I try scrubbing it with a washcloth, but it's no use. The red *BF* outline stares back at me. The last thing I need is for MaryBeth Grabowsky to see me like this.

Even though morning is slipping away, I'm not leaving my room until the marks are gone. If Kebsie were here, she'd know what to do. She was an expert at stuff like this. I remember how she used some of Shirley's makeup to disguise a bruise I got last year when I fell from the oak tree my parents told me not to climb.

I rummage through the things on my dresser, searching for something to make the redness go away, but all I have is a mess of papers and some colored pencils. Instead of staring at my blotchy face, I decide to write Kebsie a letter.

My nana gave me fancy writing paper for my birthday. I was supposed to write letters to my Great-Aunt Lil, who moved to a nursing home in Holbrook. Since I never have much to say to Aunt Lil, I have a ton of it left over. Kebsie is worth the special paper.

I pull out a pale yellow sheet from the middle of the pile and begin to write.

> *Dear Kebsie,*
>
> *Guess what? MaryBeth Grabowsky got another Barbie doll. It could be one of those talking ones. I'm not sure. If it is, I suspect I'll find out soon enough. You know MaryBeth. She's probably strutting around Ramble Street showing off her stupid dolls this very second. I hope she drops all 13 of them in the mud.*
>
> *I got through the end of 5th grade without you. But on the last day of school, Mrs. Webber glared down at me and said that even without my partner in crime, I was still trouble. I think*

*she meant you. I always thought I should be
your partner in crime, since you had all the
great ideas.*

*Remember that charm that you made me get
the day we rode our bicycles to the candy store?
Not the Beatles one you bought with your own
money, but the BF charms that we both got.
Well, you forgot yours when you moved.*

*I wouldn't have gotten one, especially if I'd
known that you'd leave yours at the bottom of
a closet. I told you it was corny anyway.*

From your bf,

Tamara

To tell the truth, I feel silly writing a letter. Kebsie was
an in-person friend and not a pen pal friend. Instead of
scribbling messages on paper, I should be able to march
down the street and talk to her face-to-face.

I read my note again and add a quick P.S.

*How come you didn't even tell me you were
moving? How come you didn't call me or write?*

All those days I spent with Kebsie, she never mentioned
her mother, even once. *My* mom, Shirley, was a favorite
topic of conversation.

Whenever I complained about Shirley's soap opera obsessions and burned TV dinners, Kebsie would talk about her foster grandmother, Mrs. Kutchner.

Personally, I never thought Kebsie had much to complain about. Mrs. Kutchner makes lemon drop cookies, has a pocketbook full of Pep-O-Mint Life Savers, and knows as much about baseball as Mr. Grabowsky.

I stick the letter and the *BF* charm in the envelope. I scribble on the back.

I still have mine. This one is yours. No sense in my having two of them.

By the time I finish writing the last word, I am so filled up with emptiness that my eyes grow blurry. I push everything inside me. The tears. The empty feeling. I seal up my misery the same way that I seal the envelope. No sense in getting all weepy about a girl who didn't even tell me where she was going.

When I get to where I write the address, I stop.

I don't know where to send it. All I can do is stare at a blank envelope.

CHAPTER SIX

The Battle of Life

"TAMARA ANN SIMPSON! Are you going to sleep all day or are you going to help me with some vacuuming?" Shirley calls from downstairs. "Come on, Tamara, we're burning daylight."

I jam the note into my back pocket and hurry to the living room, where my mother is dusting in one place. The rest of the furniture is still grimy, but the table in front of the TV is spotless.

"Are we having company?" I ask. Shirley only cleans for a reason.

"Your brother is coming home this weekend," she says as she throws a dust rag at me.

I catch it with one hand. "When?"

"You know your brother. He never tells us anything. But he said that it might be next Friday, as soon as his final exams are done."

I try to remember the last time I saw Tim. Maybe it was last Christmas. No wonder Shirley's starting her cleaning frenzy early.

"Hey, Mom, did you hear anything about Kebsie?"

"Who?" Shirley picks up another rag, but her eyes are glued to the TV, where a man dressed in a jumpsuit is counting out jumping jacks. "One and two and three and four."

I should know better not to begin conversations when Shirley is watching Jack LaLanne.

"What's he doing now?" I ask, knowing full well that she'll have to tell me about her program before she'll answer my question. I nod and pretend to be interested while Shirley explains how Jack can do push-ups using only his fingertips and how he says it's important to stop sitting around on your gluteus maximus.

I gotta hand it to him. Jack LaLanne has muscles. *Real ones*.

As soon as he's finished his deep knee bends, he straddles a wooden chair and faces the camera, looking very serious. "I have a story to tell."

Shirley motions me to be quiet even though I hadn't said a word.

Jack continues, "You know, I like to think of life as a

battlefield. Every morning when we open our eyes and wake up, we have a battle on our hands . . ."

"Isn't he handsome?" Shirley sighs.

"I guess." I shrug.

"So many people are unhappy because they have lost the battle of life," says Jack.

"The battle of life," says Shirley. "Isn't that clever?"

"I guess."

"Either life is working for you or you're working for life," says Jack.

"Working for life." Shirley repeats his words.

Jack ends his talk with an "Okay, you with me? Good." And Shirley sighs.

When the show is over, I ask again, "Do you know what happened to Kebsie Grobser? The girl who moved away?"

"I told you about asking those poor children about their background. It's not polite and it's none of your business why they have to live in foster care." Shirley adjusts the rabbit ears on top of the television set. "You don't question them, do you?"

"Never," I say through gritted teeth. "But MaryBeth said that Kebsie moved back with her mother."

"I suppose Mrs. Kutchner would know."

"She didn't know much the day Kebsie moved away. All she said was that Kebsie didn't live there anymore." I stare at the commercial on TV. A knight on a white horse is zapping dirty laundry with his lance.

Shirley sprays some lemony wax on the coffee table. "Sometimes when grown-ups speak to you, Tamara, you have a way of turning them off." She wipes the wax with a rag. "Did you listen to what Mrs. Kutchner said?"

"When she told me about Kebsie?" I say.

Shirley nods.

Of course, I didn't listen. Not one bit. When you go over to your best friend's house expecting to spend the afternoon playing Bobby Sherman records and instead you find out she's moved away for good, you're too busy trying to figure out how to hold back those deep, heavy sobs to listen to the details.

I answer with a shrug.

"Maybe you should ask Mrs. Kutchner again. Maybe she has some more information," says Shirley.

I'm not sure if she means this very minute, but I run outside before Shirley can protest.

Even though I've knocked on Mrs. Kutchner's door a hundred times before, something about this time feels strange.

Instead of Kebsie, Muscle Man's older brother Greg appears. He grunts hello, and I wonder if he's staring at the *BF* mark.

"Can I speak to Mrs. Kutchner?" I put my hand over my face to hide my cheek.

He grunts again and leaves me outside.

A few minutes later, Mrs. Kutchner comes to the door.

"Hello, Tamara."

"I want to ask you about Kebsie."

"Come in." She leads me to the living room. I work my way around the table full of knickknacks and flop onto the couch. The plastic slipcover squeaks.

In the forty-three days since I've been here, nothing much has changed. I look around for the statue of the old lady holding a small child, the one that Kebsie and I broke during a pillow fight. We glued it together before Mrs. Kutchner found out about it.

I find it, tucked in the back behind a statue of a man riding a horse and a collection of baby elephants. But even from far away, I can see the crack and the dried-up glue. I wonder if Mrs. Kutchner noticed.

"I want to know what happened to Kebsie."

Mrs. Kutchner shifts in her chair. "Kebsie is back with her mother now. They moved away. I don't know where she is."

I stare down at the letter I have in my hands. When I look up, Muscle Man's standing in front of me.

"Hiya, Tammy." He grins.

"Douglas, would you be a dear and pour Tamara and me a glass of lemonade?" asks Mrs. Kutchner.

"Sure, Grandma," he says. Grandma. That's another lie. All of the foster kids call her that.

Mrs. Kutchner waits to hear the clinking of the lemonade glasses before she continues. "Tamara, I'm sorry. I don't know where she is. They're starting over. And it's best that we don't know where they are."

"But I have a letter . . ."

"Tamara, honey, did Kebsie ever mention her father? And what he did to her?"

Neither parent. Never. I shake my head.

"He hurt them both. They don't want him to find them, so they didn't tell anyone where they were going. That's why we don't know."

"But I have a letter," I say again.

Mrs. Kutchner pats my hand. "She might contact you when they both feel safe, honey. I gave her your address."

"It's been forty-three days."

Muscle Man returns juggling three glasses of lemonade in his sweaty hands.

The sight of him standing there makes Mrs. Kutchner change her tone. "Thank you, Douglas. Isn't that nice that Douglas is here now?" she asks, as if Kebsie Grobser and Muscle Man were interchangeable. Well, maybe to an old lady like Mrs. Kutchner a slippery, slimy, lying weasel of a boy can replace Kebsie Grobser, but not to me.

I leave without touching the lemonade, but Muscle Man is right behind me.

"Tamara, wait!" he says before I get to the curb. I keep going. There's nothing he can say that would make me turn around.

"I know how to get a letter to Kebsie," he shouts, and I stop dead in my tracks.

"Mrs. Swanson, who's my caseworker, she was Kebsie's too, I bet."

"You were listening to my conversation with Mrs. Kutchner?"

"I didn't mean to. But I can help."

I decide it's worth giving Muscle Man ten seconds of my time. "Can you really get her a letter?"

"Mrs. Swanson and I are good friends. The best. She'll get the letter to Kebsie. Give it to me." He holds out his grubby hands.

I pull away.

If Jack LaLanne is right about life being a battlefield, then Muscle Man is the enemy. And there is no way I am going to hand over Kebsie's letter to the enemy. I hold the letter tight, close to me.

"Come on, Tammy, there's no other way," he says. His hands are still outstretched.

I didn't have a choice. Not handing the letter over meant that I'd never hear from Kebsie again.

For Kebsie, I'd do it. Kebsie was worth the trouble.

I shove the letter at him and head for home.

CHAPTER SEVEN

Banned

I CAN NEVER count on my mother to answer the door when her soap operas are on. Even though Shirley is sitting in the living room, just ten steps away from the front door, I race downstairs from my bedroom as soon as I hear a knock. Kebsie has been gone for forty-five days now, and I wonder if it's her.

Instead, I find John Marcos, Big Danny, and Billy Rattle standing on the stoop. Muscle Man worms his way in between them. "Hiya, Tammy." He smiles, but the others are much more serious.

MaryBeth Grabowsky is outside too, keeping her distance, pacing up and down on the sidewalk, wringing her hands and looking pouty. Benny Schuster is walking alongside her and so is one of the Donovan twins, although I'm not sure which one.

"You have to come outside," says John Marcos.

"I'll be right back," I call to Shirley. She's way too interested in *The Days of Our Lives* to answer.

As soon as we walk over to the Grabowsky's front lawn, I know what's going on. "Does someone have a gripe?" I ask.

When John Marcos answers, "Yes," I am not surprised. The only time we're allowed on the Grabowsky's lawn is when we are doing quiet activities like talking. And the only reason for talking is when someone has a gripe.

We tiptoe through the grass, taking special care not to dig in with our heels and scuff up the lawn. Mr. Grabowsky hates scuff marks.

I keep a careful eye on Billy Rattle to make sure he's on his toes. Last year Kebsie and I got blamed for some grass getting pulled up when I'm sure it was caused by Billy running over the lawn wearing baseball cleats. "You'd better be careful," I tell him.

I flop down on the ground, and I have to admit that it does feel nicer than Shirley's dandelion patch. As soon as I catch MaryBeth watching me run my hands over the cushiony tufts of grass, I stop. I wouldn't want MaryBeth Grabowsky to know that I think her lawn looks nice.

Whenever someone has a gripe, the first thing we do is gather on the lawn and form a circle. MaryBeth sits down, like she usually does, with Benny Schuster on one side and the Donovan twin on the other. The moment John Marcos takes his place in the center, MaryBeth gives him a smile. At least he doesn't smile back.

Of all places, Muscle Man flops down next to me, right where Kebsie used to sit. "Is anyone else coming?" he asks.

"We called for everyone. No one else is around," says John Marcos.

"Not a single Marchetta kid?" asks Billy Rattle. With eleven children in the family, normally there's at least one of them floating around.

"They're all too busy swimming in their new pool," explains Big Danny, who lives next door to them.

"Your brother coming?" I ask the Donovan twin.

"He's at the dentist." He grins.

Benny Schuster gives the twin a light slap on the head. "Quit smiling likes it's a good thing."

Big Danny spies Tony Mogavero riding down the street on his bicycle. Two punky kids, who are strangers, ride with him. Big Danny waves, but Tony shakes his head and peddles away, his punky friends at his side.

"It's been like that ever since he transferred to Catholic school," says the Donovan twin. "I guess he thinks he's too good for us."

I nod. "Yeah, I noticed."

A few weeks ago, I asked Tony if he wanted to play kickball. And even though he is the best outfielder we've ever had, he shrugged it off as if the game meant nothing to him.

I've had a hard time liking him ever since.

"We're ready," says John Marcos.

I've never been clear on how John got the job of running the gripe votes, but he's been doing it every summer for as long as I can remember. And except for when I don't agree with him, he does a pretty good job at it.

I look around, wondering whose head is on the chopping block. On Ramble Street, you have to be careful. The slightest misbehavior can get you ousted from a game. And there is no point to summer if you can't play kickball.

"I would like to begin," says Billy Rattle. Then he jingles the change in his pockets to show he means business.

As soon as he gets the nod from John Marcos, Billy Rattle makes his big announcement. "Big Danny stole money from me."

Big Danny jumps to his feet. "No way! I found that money over by the railroad tracks."

John Marcos orders Big Danny to be quiet and lets Billy Rattle tell everyone how he lost fifty cents and how it was an awfully odd coincidence that Big Danny found the exact same amount that very same day.

Big Danny explains over and over again how he found the money by the railroad tracks and asks Billy if the fifty cents that he lost was in quarters, nickels, or dimes.

"Two quarters. Five dimes. Who remembers? I have so much change, I forget," says Billy Rattle.

Like most kids with money, Billy knows when to flaunt it. When he shakes his pockets again, a bunch of change falls to the ground. The sight of all those nickels, dimes, and quarters scattered on the lawn blocks out anything sensible that Big Danny has to say.

Big Danny looks worried. And who could blame him? To be accused of stealing? That could get you banned from kickball for days.

John Marcos stands up, and I figure he's going to say that it's time to put this money thing to a vote. Instead he nods at Benny Schuster. "Now for the second order of business."

I look around to see who's next.

Benny grabs at MaryBeth's arm. "Look what Tammy did to MaryBeth," he says, waving her arm back and forth like a flag.

The Donovan twin leans over. "That looks bad."

Everyone, even John Marcos, rushes over to take a look.

I spring up to see for myself. On MaryBeth Grabowsky's dainty little arm there is a tiny, faint bruise, one that I have to squint to block out the sun to see.

"When?" I demand.

"Yesterday when we were playing, you pushed her to

the ground," says the Donovan twin, and I wish I could remember which one he is so I know exactly who I'll be carrying a grudge against for the rest of my born days.

"She was standing on the baseline. I was running for third." I point my finger at MaryBeth. "It's her fault. No fielder is allowed to stand on a baseline. There are rules about being in the way."

As soon as I see that solemn look on John Marco's face, I realize that we are looking at MaryBeth's arm for a reason. "Wait a minute! You're going to vote? On a little thing like an accidental shove?"

"It didn't seem like an accident to me," says Billy Rattle. "And it hurt, didn't it, MaryBeth?"

Rubbing her arm for effect, MaryBeth nods. And the boys gather around MaryBeth Grabowsky like they always do.

"*I* should be the one who has a gripe against *her*. *She* was in the way." I kick my foot into the ground to emphasize my point.

A large chunk of sod comes flying off the lawn. There is a big brown spot where the grass should be. Mr. Grabowsky's perfect lawn is ruined.

"Look what you did!" MaryBeth glances toward her front door and back at the spot in the middle of the grass. The other kids gather around it. The way everyone is staring, you'd think the hole was as big as the Grand Canyon.

I pick up the sod, and I'm surprised at how heavy it is.

The chunk in my hands is pretty big.

Muscle Man moves the dirt around. "I'm an expert gardener. Give the sod to me. I'll fix it. No one will ever know."

"Nice going, Tamara," says Billy Rattle. "You messed up the lawn." He jingles the change in his pockets. "Come on everyone, let's get back to the gripes. I'm ready to vote."

I don't stay around while Billy Rattle, Muscle Man McGinty, and the others on Ramble Street decide my fate. I run away, taking the chunk of sod with me, leaving the others to gape at the big brown spot in the middle of Mr. Grabowsky's lawn.

CHAPTER EIGHT

The Fourth of July

"HEY MUSCLE MAN," I grunt. It kills me to say hello to the kid, but I have no choice. I've been standing alone at the Fourth of July barbeque for over an hour now. No one else is talking to me.

"Why hello, Tammy." A stupid grin is smashed across his face. "This is a real nice party. Don't you think?"

I shrug. Billy Rattle's parents always have a July 4th barbeque. To me, it looks the same as last year's and the year before that. A bunch of neighbors. Hamburgers. Hot Dogs. Sparklers. Mr. Rattle's accordion playing. Pretty standard stuff.

"Is MaryBeth still mad at me?" I ask, even though I'm

not sure why I care. I did nothing wrong, and she's just being stupid.

"Oh gosh, I hope not," he says.

A group of neighbors on the other side of the yard is getting ready to do the bunny hop. MaryBeth Grabowsky is in the middle of the crowd, jumping up and down, practicing her bunny steps. I try to catch her eye.

When she sees me, she throws me a dirty look and hops to the other side of the line.

"Did you play kickball today?" I ask.

Muscle Man nods. "It wasn't the same without you, Tammy. Too bad you couldn't play."

I wonder if Muscle Man is rubbing it in. It's not like I didn't *want* to play. As I expected, I was banned.

"What happened with Big Danny?" I ask. "Was he banned too?"

"Two days, same as you, and a few kids called him a thief."

I shake my head. "Big Danny is not a thief."

"For the record, when we voted about you, I voted to let you play," says Muscle Man. "After all, you were the one who gave me my name."

For a moment, I'm not sure if he means it or if he's being sarcastic. "You *like* your name?"

"Sure." He nods. "I think it fits me good."

In truth, I think it fits him too. But not in the same way

he does. After all, what else can you call a kid who goes around bragging that he's the bravest, smartest, strongest, fastest person who ever graced the planet?

"They'll let you play tomorrow. You were only banned for two days," he says.

"Yeah, you know how it is when they ban you. It never lasts for long," I say.

Muscle Man nods, and I realize that this is another one of his falsehoods. The kid has no idea of what I'm talking about. As far as I know, Muscle Man McGinty has never gotten ousted from a kickball game. Not even once.

And on Ramble Street, *that* is something to brag about.

Muscle Man turns to leave, but I step in front of him. "Just a minute. You never told me what happened with the letter. Did you hear anything?"

Muscle Man ignores me. He waves hello to Mrs. Murphy, who's sitting alone in a corner, wrestling with a giant piece of Mrs. Rattle's Fourth of July pie. "Hi, Mrs. Murphy. How are your roses growing? Did you get rid of those mealy worms?"

Mrs. Murphy, a cranky old lady who hasn't cracked a smile since November of 1963, giggles. "The roses are doing well. The worms are gone. How nice of you to ask about them."

"Did I ever tell you about the mealy worms in my old garden?" begins Muscle Man, but I won't let him finish his tale.

"What happened with the letter?" I interrupt. "Can your caseworker get it to Kebsie? Will she write back?"

Before he can answer, a cheer goes through the crowd.

"We want Pizza! We want Pizza! We want Pizzarelli to sing!"

Mr. Pizzarelli, who always takes this day off from his job as a police officer, pretends to be surprised. To get the crowd going, Mr. Rattle plays the accordion in time with the chants. "Peet-zah! Peet-zah!"

"What's happening?" asks Muscle Man.

"Never mind what's happening. What about the letter?" I yell, but my words are drowned out by the noise.

Mr. Pizzarelli jumps up after the crowd is worked into a frenzy. He holds up his hands, and the crowd goes quiet.

I lean toward Muscle Man. "The letter?" I whisper. But before I can say anything else, a dozen people shush me at once. I turn around and see Mrs. Murphy, her lips pursed in shushing position, waiting for me to speak again.

I sit down on the grass next to Muscle Man and listen to Mr. Pizzarelli sing. After he does a few solo numbers, a few of the neighbors join him. By the time Mr. Pizzarelli gets to "This Land Is Your Land" and "God Bless America," most everyone on Ramble Street is singing.

But the last song belongs to Mr. Pizzarelli. He always ends with his favorite, "If I Were a Rich Man." It brings the house down. This year, he gives his best performance.

As soon as he finishes crooning his last "bid de bid de

bum" and before the neighbors can call out for an encore, Muscle Man is at his side.

"Hey, Mr. Pizza. Great voice. You really know how to work a crowd. Did I ever tell you about the time I sang on Broadway? Let me know if you ever need some pointers on how to hit those high notes."

For a moment, I think that Muscle Man is finally going to get his due. You'd think that a cop would be able to spot a fib and that there'd be a special penalty for lying to a police officer (maybe one that involves handcuffs). But Mr. Pizzarelli only smiles at him and heads over to the line of people who are getting ready to dance the Alley Cat.

Muscle Man tugs at my arm. "Come on, Tammy. Let's dance."

I plant my feet firmly into the ground. "Forget about it."

Muscle Man races toward the Alley Cat line, and I race after him. He's not getting away this easy.

When we reach the group, Mr. Rattle is instructing the dancers. "Hop. Skip. Turn. And then you all shout, 'Meow.'" He plays a few notes on his accordion and the dance begins.

Muscle Man is three steps behind the others, twisting and hopping like no alley cat I ever saw. I wave my hands in front of his face, but he turns and dances in a new direction.

The music stops, and suddenly I'm shouting, "What about Kebsie?"

Muscle Man, whose hands are held up like paws in alley cat position, struggles to catch his breath.

I move in front of him. This time he's not getting away. "Did you give the caseworker the letter?"

Finally, he nods. "Yup, you should be hearing from Kebsie soon."

CHAPTER NINE

When You Can't Eat Ice Cream, Eat Your Words

"Don't drip on me," Billy Rattle warns Big Danny. It's Big Danny's and my first day back after being banned, and Billy Rattle is still grinning from his victory about the fifty cents.

We're crammed elbow to elbow on the front stoop of the Grabowsky house, and Big Danny is eating his usual, a Mr. Softee double black and white twist, so Billy Rattle has good reason for worrying about drips.

Only two of us didn't buy anything when the truck came around. Me and Muscle Man sit empty-handed, watching the others slurp down their cones.

It's a sun-melting-tar kind of afternoon, and I bet that ice cream tastes good. Muscle Man is probably thinking the same thing. I can tell by the way he eyes the drops that land on the sidewalk.

The other kids don't notice the two of us staring at their cones like they're worth a million bucks. They have other things on their minds.

"What if the moon is gooey and soft? What if the astronauts get swallowed up as soon as they walk on it?" Big Danny never takes his eyes off of his swirly cone. "The surface of the moon could be as mushy as ice cream."

"Impossible," says John Marcos. He grabs a napkin and wipes his hands. For a boy, John is neat. "You have ice cream on your brain."

"John's right," chimes in MaryBeth Grabowsky. "My uncle works for Grumman. He helped build the LEM. He says the moon is as hard as a rock."

"Your uncle has something to do with the first moon walk?" I notice that she and John are sitting real close. "Yeah, right."

"What's the matter with you, Tammy?" Billy Rattle smirks. "Don't you know that the LEM was built a few miles away from here in Bethpage?"

When it comes to brains, Billy Rattle is a few marshmallow candies short of a bowl of Lucky Charms. It bothers me that he seems to suddenly know so much about the moon walk. Especially since I don't.

"You don't even know what the LEM is, do you?"

John Marcos looks me straight in the eye, and it's as if he's reading my mind.

"'LEM' stands for 'Lunar Excursion Module'. That's the name of the craft that's going to separate from the *Apollo 11* spaceship and land on the moon," says Billy Rattle, of all people.

"Don't you remember last week when MaryBeth's uncle came over and told us all about it?" asks John Marcos.

MaryBeth beams when John mentions her name, and I wish her eyes weren't such a deep shade of turquoise.

"I wasn't there," I mutter.

"Were you grounded?" asks MaryBeth. "You're always grounded."

The others snicker.

Muscle Man pushes his way between Big Danny and me. "I have an uncle who is the boss of MaryBeth's uncle. He runs the whole thing. The LEM. The moonwalk. The works."

"Oh, yeah?" Now, it's my turn to snicker. "What's his name?"

Muscle Man doesn't skip a beat. "Neil Armstrong. My uncle is Neil Armstrong, the astronaut."

"Yeah, right. Your uncle is the head of the *Apollo 11* mission." I say the words loud and slow so the others in the group understand exactly how tall this tale is getting. "Neil Armstrong, the man who's gonna be the first person to walk on the moon, is your uncle?"

"Uncle Neil," nods Muscle Man. "He's like a father to me."

The others in the group turn away. Billy Rattle shreds his napkin into tiny pieces. Big Danny stares down at his shoe. MaryBeth plays with her shiny hair, and John Marcos swats a mosquito. I try, but I can't make eye contact with a single one of them.

"Like a father," I huff. "Jeez."

"My parents are going to let me stay up late and watch the whole thing," says Billy Rattle, his lips blue from his berry Italian ice.

"Me too," chimes in just about everyone else.

I keep my mouth shut. I doubt there's a chance of my staying up that late for anything. My parents would never go for it.

There's no need to say any more. The ice cream is finished. The talking is done.

John Marcos picks up the ball and bounces it two or three times on the sidewalk. "You ready?" He nods to the gang.

We head toward Billy Rattle's house. In the summer, his front lawn is known as "the field."

Muscle Man stays behind. "I think I'll sit this one out." He yawns. "I'm kind of tired."

"Maybe you can go call Uncle Neil and see how things are going with the blastoff." I have to add more. "You're not tired. More like you stink at kickball, and you don't want to play."

"That's not true, Tammy. I'm a good player," he says, with his fake smile.

Muscle Man never gets angry when I challenge him, and it burns me to bits.

"You're the worst player on the block." I can't let it go. Instead, I do a nasty imitation of Muscle Man trying to kick the ball.

John Marcos gives me a sharp elbow, MaryBeth Grabowsky sighs, and Billy Rattle's blue lips start to move. But whatever Billy is planning to say, he never gets a chance. Muscle Man cuts him off.

"Come on, Tammy, you know that's not true." Nothing stops Muscle Man when he's on a roll. Right then and there, Muscle Man utters the stupidest words that any kid has ever said.

"I'm the best player on Ramble Street. I could take you on, all at once, if I wanted to."

Five mouths drop open at the same time.

Billy Rattle bangs the side of his own head. I don't blame the kid. I'm wondering myself if my hearing's gone screwy.

Kickball is our game. No, it is more than a game. It is sacred.

On Ramble Street, tough talk about kickball cannot be ignored.

There's only one thing to do.

John Marcos closes his fists. "Prove it!"

"Name the date and time," says Muscle Man.

"Tomorrow morning. Ten o'clock," says Big Danny. The others nod.

"I'll be there," Muscle Man says with a grin, but I bet that behind that crooked smile is a barrelful of regret. On the outside, he looks cool, but inside, he has to be shaking. After all, he just challenged the entire block to our favorite game.

A delicious feeling creeps into me, like I'm suddenly filled with dozens of Mr. Softee's swirly cones. It's the day I've been waiting for. No more stupid grin. No more slimy words. This time he crossed the line. And he's going to pay for it.

Tomorrow, Muscle Man McGinty is going down.

CHAPTER TEN

Secret Powers

THERE ARE LUCKY people in the world, and then there are people who always seem to find themselves knee-deep in trouble. It's not hard to guess which group I fall into.

If I were lucky, the morning of the us-against-Muscle Man game would be different. I'd wake up to singing birds and sunshine, scarf down a bowl of Apple Jacks, and be the first one standing on the Rattle's front lawn.

But I'm a "trouble" person. And that means I'm in deep water from the moment the day begins. First, there are no Apple Jacks. Shirley forgot to buy cereal. "That stuff will rot out your teeth." She reaches for a cigarette. "Here, eat this instead."

I stare at the plate of eggs she plops down in front of me. They're cold and runny.

"Can I go out and play?"

"You're not wandering around the neighborhood in this rain." Shirley waves her hand at the window, and I have to admit I can't see a thing but gray sheets of water.

"But Mom, there's a big game today," I protest. "Everyone is going to be there." The rest of the kids will find a way out of their houses, I'm sure of it. After all, this is important. A little rain is nothing compared to honor.

"Besides, Tim is coming home," she says, "and this time I want things to be nice."

I play with the yolks while my mother rattles off chores that need to be done. When she finishes, I try again. "The game won't last long. It's just a morning thing."

My mother isn't budging. And I begin to worry that the game could go on without me.

Shirley takes a can of lemony stuff and sprays it all over the kitchen counters. "Come on, Tammy, let's get this place looking nice for Tim."

"A lot of good it's going to do." I point to the den where Marshall is holed up with the morning paper. "They're still going to argue."

Shirley scrubs the counter. "No, your father's promised and so has Tim."

"Yeah, right. Until they see each other in person. Then

the fireworks will start." I act out the scene from the last time Tim was home, using a deep bellowing voice for Marshall. "When are you going to get a job, Tim?"

And a medium voice for Tim. "Dad, you work for 'the man.'"

And then I go back to Marshall's bellow. "Mr. Rendizzi is not 'the man.'"

Before I use the medium voice, I roll my eyes, the exact way that Tim does. Then in my best imitation of my brother, I say, "Dad, you work for big business. That's 'the man.' And all 'the man' cares about is making money off of the little people."

"That is enough, Tamara," says Shirley, and I can tell by the way that she glares at me that I'm exactly two seconds away from getting grounded.

Big Danny is right. I'm always getting punished for doing practically nothing. All I did was try to remind my mother that a sparkling kitchen cannot stop my brother and father from fighting.

"I'll clean up downstairs," I volunteer. It's one of her main gripes. The basement serves as a combination of laundry room and Tim's room. It's always a mess.

Shirley takes a drag of her cigarette and waves me away. "Put a load of laundry up while you're down there."

I grab a basket, throw in some dirty towels, and hop

down to the basement as fast as I can. Nothing's keeping me away from that game, not even Shirley.

There isn't really anything in the basement to clean. Most of the books, records, and concert souvenirs belong to Tim. He took the place over before he went away to college. In his senior year of high school, he even slept down here.

I turn on the washing machine and wait for the water to fill. I stare at Tim's poster of Jimi Hendrix.

The poster is falling off the wall, one side of it curls down from the dampness. I find some tape and stick it back as best I can.

I decide that it's time to use my special powers. I sink into Grandma's old rocking chair, the one we keep in the basement because everyone thinks it's ugly. And I summon Tim.

"Tim telephone. Tim telephone. Tim telephone." Faster and faster I chant, until it sounds like it's all one word. "Timtelephone. Timtelephone. Timtelephone."

Nine times out of ten, Tim will call if I try real hard.

When it doesn't happen right away, I think about something special about him. Today, I think about the time Tim taught me how to climb the big oak tree. The trick is to step on the chopped-off limb with your left foot and swing over with your right. When he still doesn't call, I think about how he spends hours in the basement listening to music and how he says Jimi Hendrix's guitar playing makes him feel restless. When that doesn't work, I stare long and hard at the picture of Tim and his best friend, Vinnie Pizzarelli. I wipe off a thin layer of dust until I can see them both, smiling back at me.

The phone rings.

I listen for Shirley to pick it up. I can tell by the way she says hello that it's Tim.

I lean back into the chair and sigh. My special powers worked again.

After a while, Shirley calls down the stairs and tells me to pick up the phone.

I grab the one by Tim's desk. "I got it," I shout to Shirley.

Both Tim and I wait for her to hang up before we speak.

"Hiya, Beanpole. Did you will me to call?"

"Yep."

Tim laughs. "Just make sure you use your secret powers for good, okay?"

"They only work with you. I've tried them a million other times and nothing." A million and one is more like it. I've willed and chanted and wished until I turned blue. I've tried for no homework. A snow day. A new bicycle. Ice cream for dinner. And, of course, I've been willing Kebsie to call for forty-seven days now. My special powers are very limited.

"The parents treating you okay?" Tim asks.

"Shirley and Marshall are treating me fine," I say, just so I can say their names out loud.

"Shirley? And Marshall?" Tim laughs. "Is that what you're calling them now?"

"Not exactly to their faces," I explain.

Tim laughs again.

"Are you coming home this weekend?" I ask.

"I meant to, but I'm really busy. I'm taking a summer class, and then there's a big concert upstate. It's gonna last for days, and I really want to go."

I kick at the nearby table. The picture of Vinnie and Tim goes crashing to the floor. "Does that mean that you won't be home all summer?" I ask.

"Jimi Hendrix will be performing there," he says, as if that explains everything. When I don't say anything, he adds, "Everyone will be there."

"Be there or be square, right?" I say, because it's Tim's favorite expression. I'm never quite sure where "there" is, but in Tim's book, the worst thing you can be is an out-of-touch "square."

There's a sharp crackle of static, and I'm reminded that Tim is calling long distance.

"Hey, Beanpole. I finally got a letter from Vinnie. Can you tell Mr. Pizzarelli that? He says he's doing okay. That things have quieted down."

I pick up the picture of Vinnie and Tim and rub my hand against the glass, checking it for damage. It was taken two years ago in front of Vinnie's first car, back when Vinnie Pizzarelli didn't have a care in the world, before his number came up in the draft.

"Is he still your best friend?" I ask, without really thinking.

"What?"

I take a big gulp and ask again. "Is Vinnie Pizzarelli still your best friend?" I want to know.

"Of course. Jeez, Tamara, he's thousands of miles away from home, fighting a war. If anyone needs a friend, it's a guy who's over in Vietnam."

"Even if he doesn't write to you?"

"He's in a war, for Pete's sake. He can't write all the time. His letters are like gold to me. And to his dad, too. That's why it's important for you to go tell Mr. Pizzarelli about the letter. Tell him I'll bring it the next time I come home. Promise me you'll go see Mr. Pizzarelli?"

"Yes." I rub my hand along the picture and make a point to touch Vinnie's face. "I promise."

"Even when someone is far away, they don't stop being your best friend, Beanpole." There's more static. "Ah look, I gotta go."

He hangs up and leaves me with nothing but his and Vinnie's picture and a basement full of the empty feeling of missing Kebsie. Funny about how talking about Tim and his best friend makes me lonely for mine.

I reach for the box of Oreos Tim keeps stashed in his top drawer and shove one into my mouth.

"Even though you are far away, Kebsie Grobser," I whisper, "you will never stop being my best friend."

I stare at the picture of my brother and his friend, wishing it were of Kebsie and me. We didn't have anything like it. There were group pictures at birthday parties, but I didn't have one of just the two of us.

I shut my eyes and imagine the picture is of me and Kebsie. I have the perfect image of us eating hot dogs on the field trip to Teddy Roosevelt's house. That day, Kebsie plopped herself down at the picnic table and did imitations of Mrs. Webber. When I was the only one who laughed, Kebsie told me I was cool. That was the moment I decided I liked her better than anyone.

I hold the picture close and try real hard to burn the image of me and Kebsie into its frame. When I open my eyes, Vinnie and Tim are still staring at me, smiling in front of Vinnie's car.

My secret powers need work.

CHAPTER ELEVEN

Just My Luck

A CLAP OF thunder makes me jump. I glance at the clock on the wall. It's 10:05, a whole five minutes after game time. By now, the other kids are probably standing around waiting for me. After all, I am the pitcher.

The basement has a door leading to the outside. If I open it right, slow but steady, I can avoid it making a groan, and Shirley will never know I'm gone.

I run straight through the puddles that have gathered on the sidewalk. Soon I'm standing on the Rattles' front lawn.

I am alone.

The sight of the empty field knocks the wind out of me, just like when John Marcos accidentally kicked a low-flying ball straight into my stomach two summers ago. But that breathless feeling from the ball went away after a few minutes. This one stays with me, growing deeper with each new crack of thunder.

No one else cared enough to come. A few measly thunderbolts and some flashes of lightning kept them all away.

I glare up and down the block, searching for a sign that someone will join me. But the street is empty. I pay special attention to the old house right across the street, where Muscle Man lives.

Talk about luck. He couldn't have planned better weather. The pouring rain gives him more time to figure out a way to weasel out of this.

Of all people, he should have been here. Even if no one else showed up, he should be standing in the rain along side me. He was the one who threw down the challenge.

"Come on, Muscle Man!" I shout to his house, which is shut up tight. "Right now! Come on out and show the world what you're made of!"

A rattle of thunder and a few quick flashes of lightning are my only answer.

"Let's go! You got a game to play!"

The ball sits in a puddle by first base, exactly where John Marcos threw it down the night before. I pick it up and bounce it a few times.

At the next house over, a door opens. Mrs. Grabowsky steps outside. "Tammy, sweetie, go home. No one is playing today."

"Oh, no. You're wrong, Mrs. Grabowsky. They're just late, but they're coming." I bounce the ball again. It makes a *splat* sound against a puddle.

"Go home. You'll catch your death of cold," she says.

"Is MaryBeth coming out?" I pop up the ball with my knee and catch it on the way down.

Mrs. Grabowsky shakes her head. "No, MaryBeth is not coming out."

"Too bad. Tell her she's going to miss a good game."

"Tamara Ann Simpson, if you don't go home this minute, I'm going to call your mother."

It figures. That's what happens when you're a trouble person. People pick on you for doing nothing. All I'm doing is minding my own business, waiting for the game to start.

I slam the ball into the biggest puddle I can find. It sends water flying up so hard that even I jump.

"You'd better be out here tomorrow, Muscle Man, or I'll come and get you," I shout across the street with Mrs. Grabowsky watching me.

"I mean it, Tamara. This is your last chance." Mrs. Grabowsky has her hands on her hips now, and I know I don't have much time left.

Before she can make any phone calls, I head home.

I stay down in the basement for most of the day, listening to Tim's Jimi Hendrix records and doing laundry, anything to keep away from Shirley.

Every so often I sneak back outside and glance down the block at the Rattle's front lawn. But the only thing gathering on Ramble Street is a bunch of puddles.

CHAPTER TWELVE

Let the Game Begin

WORD TRAVELS FAST on Ramble Street. Even a day of torrential rain couldn't stop the entire block from hearing about Muscle Man's challenge.

The morning after the storm, we're ready for him. At 9:30, eleven of us are standing on the Rattle's front lawn. It's been a long time since I've seen us all together.

Big Danny and John Marcos stand in the center of the group. The others swarm around them.

Tony Mogavero pedals by with those punky kids at his side. As soon as Big Danny explains the situation to him, Tony drops his bike. "Catch you later," he tells those two kids from Catholic school, and just like old times, he's back with us.

I almost get knocked over by one of the Donovan twins. He's too busy shoving his brother to even say sorry. After eleven years, Matthew and Michael Donovan haven't figured out that both of them can't occupy the same space at the same time.

"Come on, guys, cut it out." Benny Schuster is friends with both of them and probably says those words a hundred times a day.

MaryBeth floats around the crowd with her little sister, Janie Lee, showing off their matching outfits and silky hair. It reminds me that I should have at least redone my pony tail this morning.

I stand next to Conchetta Marchetta for a while. You can always count on a Marchetta to show up for a big event. Conchetta is a nice girl. Dull. But nice. I try to talk to her about summer and sprinklers and stuff, but after about thirty seconds, I run out of things to say.

By 9:50, I can't wait any longer. I work my way into the center of the crowd. "Maybe we should call for him."

"He's got ten minutes," says John Marcos. "He's not even late."

"Yes, let's be fair and give him a chance." MaryBeth bats her eyelashes at him.

"I'm always fair," I protest.

John Marcos pays no mind to either one of us. Instead he walks over to where Billy Rattle is showing off his new transistor radio.

I kill time by standing next to MaryBeth, listening to some story about that uncle of hers who works for Grumman and the *Apollo 11* mission.

"Tammy, did you hear anything I said?" she asks.

"Of course," I say, not taking my eyes off of Muscle Man's house.

"We're having a big party at my house on moon-walk night." MaryBeth puts her hands over her mouth like she's said something terribly wrong. "Oh, Tammy, I'm so sorry."

I shrug like I don't care at all. It's not like I expect an invitation. Whenever the Grabowsky's have a party, my family's not invited. Oh sure, if there's a party where they invite everyone on the entire block, we get to go. But when it comes to a house party where only certain people are invited, the Simpsons never make the grade.

MaryBeth always seems to let it slip, though, whenever her family is having a party. We never have any kind of celebration at my house. If we ever do, I've made a solemn vow that I'll accidentally let her know too.

"Oh, Tammy, are you mad?" asks MaryBeth, in a make-believe sad voice.

I shrug again and walk away from her. I end up standing next to Big Danny, who's finishing a swirly cone.

"Where'd you get that?" I ask. Mr. Softee's first drive down Ramble Street is normally after lunch.

"We 'ave a whole boonch of 'em in the freeza." His mouth is too full to say any more. "It's my 'ird one."

"Hey, what time is it?" I notice he's wearing a watch.

"Five minnuz afta." He pushes the entire rest of the cone in his mouth, and I know he's not good for answering another thing until the mess that's in his mouth goes down his throat.

I walk over to where the crowd has gathered around Billy Rattle's new radio.

"He's late," I announce to no one in particular. "We should go get him. He's probably not coming unless we do."

It's almost as if Muscle Man hears what I'm saying from across the street, because at that moment the door opens.

Muscle Man steps outside, his face plastered with that stupid smirk. His brother, Greg, steps out next to him. The two of them cross Ramble Street.

"So, I hear you're playing kickball," Greg grunts.

Except for that time at Mrs. Kutchner's front door, I've never seen Greg up close. He looks like Muscle Man, except older and without the stupid grin. Since they moved into the neighborhood, Greg is never around much. He's thirteen, old enough to ride his bike and go anywhere he wants. And I guess Ramble Street is never where he wants to be.

Big Danny and John Marcos explain things to him.

"He said he can beat all of us," I add, impatient to get to the end of the story and to see what Greg and Muscle Man are up to.

Greg gives Muscle Man a now-you-did-it glare.

"Well, if he says he can do it, then he should do it," says Greg.

Muscle Man's expression never changes, even though, in my opinion, his brother has just thrown him to a pack of hungry wolves.

"I'm gonna be on your team too," Greg adds.

I rub my hands together. Things are turning out better than I thought. His brother is on *our* team. Against Muscle Man. I begin to feel sorry for Greg at having to live with this kid.

"Let's call it. Does someone have a coin so we can flip to see who's up first?" I look straight at Billy Rattle, the money guy.

"You know, since it's all of us against one, I think that we should let this guy be up first." Greg puts his brother in a playful choke hold. Muscle Man grins.

"That seems fair," chimes in MaryBeth, and I don't know who I want to smash first. Muscle Man for his grin or MaryBeth for her stupid comment.

She's wrong, anyway. It's not fair. That's not how we do it. We always flip a coin to see who's up first. Having Muscle Man up first, without a coin flip, is not fair. He's getting special treatment.

I wait for someone to protest.

Instead John Marcos tosses me the ball. "Okay," he says to Greg, "he's up first."

I sigh and take my place on the field.

There are too many of us to play our positions, so most of the kids gather in the outfield. Three or four crowd up around second base.

I stand on the pitcher's mound and bounce the ball, waiting for everyone to get ready. I've never seen so many of us in the field at once. John Marcos gives me a nod.

It's time to begin. Good thing too, because if it takes another minute, I'm sure I'll burst. I can't wait any longer.

I take one look at Muscle Man standing in front of home plate, and I throw my first pitch.

CHAPTER THIRTEEN

Nothing to Smile About

I START WITH a line drive, fast and straight up the middle.

It goes exactly where I want it to go, right over home plate.

Muscle Man fails to give it the respect it deserves. He's so busy smiling at me that he hardly pays attention.

My pitches are nothing to smile about. They are fierce. I've pitched to the big kids and even to my brother, Tim, and Vinnie Pizza. I can tell by the way they wrinkle their foreheads and by the way they stop joking around that I've got a good arm.

This kid is practically grinning. Here he is, playing the most important game of his life, one that's sure to prove him to be a slithering liar, and he hardly seems to be trying. By the time he even attempts to kick, the ball has rolled past him.

"Strike one," shouts John Marcos.

John's official position is catcher, but he's also the unofficial umpire. John Marcos is fair, *too fair*, in my opinion. He has no problem selling his own team down the river when he thinks the other team is in the right. There are no arguments about who is safe and who is out when John Marcos is involved. His words are like gold. And he called it a strike.

"Great pitch, Tammy," shouts Muscle Man. The stupid kid doesn't even know when he's about to get trounced.

"Yeah, well if you like that one, try this one," I pitch him another. Same pitch. Straight up the middle.

Muscle Man hardly looks at the ball. He's making funny faces at little Janie Lee Grabowsky, who's over near first base.

He misses again.

"Strike two," shouts John Marcos.

"Good pitch again," says Muscle Man, and the blood inside me sizzles.

I throw another, but this one slides out of my hand and wobbles as it heads toward home plate. Not my best pitch. A little slow. Probably, the blood bubbling up inside me caused my arm to stiffen.

Muscle Man kicks it. The ball heads straight back to me. It bounces, or I'd have caught it and he'd have been out instantly.

I don't know why the kid even bothers running, because it's pretty obvious that he's toast. Before he steps off home plate, I already have the ball in my hands.

"Throw it here," shouts Billy Rattle, the first baseman. "Come on, Tammy. What's taking you so long?"

Normally, Billy Rattle and I work well together. He can catch anything I throw to him, and he never has to shout at me to do it. But this is more than a game of kickball. This is about teaching someone a very important lesson.

So, instead of sending it to Billy Rattle, I toss the ball to Janie Lee Grabowsky. She's standing not three feet away from first base. For a second, she stares at me like I made some horrible error. But as soon as she realizes what's at stake, she springs into action.

The little kid knows exactly what to do. She runs to first base and waits for him.

The humiliation is complete. Muscle Man is tagged out by a five-year-old.

I bet then and there the grin I have on my face is as stupid as Muscle Man's.

"You're out," John Marcos shouts.

I head back to the pitcher's mound, feeling like I'm the top dog at the pound. Nothing can stop me.

It's time for my tricky pitch, the one that Vinnie Pizza taught me. I throw the ball underhand, fast and strong. It heads straight toward home plate and then hits a certain patch of lawn at the last minute, causing it to zig slightly to the left. That pitch can take even the really good players by surprise. It's one of my best moves.

Muscle Man misses.

"Strike one," shouts John Marcos.

When you've spent as much time pitching as I have, you get a sense of how the game is going to go in the first few innings. The kids in Janie Lee Grabowsky's kindergarten class would have given me more problems than Muscle Man. This game is going to be a cinch.

I don't need the other twelve players to beat this kid. I can strike him out in no time. For the first time in months, my headache goes away.

Instead of pain, my head swells with joy.

I make up a little song and sing it under my breath. "Strike one. Strike one. The fun has just begun."

My next pitch is an exact replay of my last one. It always gets them, that zig. For some players, I can do it a hundred times before they learn how to kick it back. For Muscle Man, I bet I could pitch it a thousand times.

"Strike two," shouts John Marcos.

"Boy, your pitches are good today," Muscle Man gives me an enormously stupid smile. "Good job, Tammy."

"You ain't seen nothing yet!" I shout back at him.

My next pitch is perfect. Fast. Smooth. And impossible to hit.

It sails past him. He doesn't even see it.

"Strike three. Second out," says John Marcos.

Before John throws back the ball, Greg McGinty signals to him that it's time to talk. He runs over to where John Marcos stands behind home plate.

I wait.

Normally these things don't take too long, but John and Greg keep blabbing.

"Come on, guys, we're burning daylight." I turn around and look at my team, waiting for one of them to join in and back me up.

Big Danny pulls a candy bar out of his shirt pocket. MaryBeth Grabowsky plays with her hair. The Donovan twins are in left field, elbowing each other over who gets to stand in the best position. Conchetta Marchetta ties and reties her sneakers. A few other kids stare up at the sky. No one says anything about hurrying.

Greg points to Muscle Man. A few times John Marcos shakes his head and waves his hands around. I try to lean in to listen, but their conversation is soft. I can't hear a word.

I think about joining them. I'm the pitcher after all, and I'm entitled to walk over there to see what's up, but to be honest, I'm a little scared of Greg McGinty.

He's big. He grunts. He's Muscle Man's older brother, and he can probably tell in a heartbeat that Muscle Man's mere existence causes me grief.

A dozen years go by before Greg McGinty heads back to the field, and John Marcos walks over to me.

"Take it easy on him." John looks at the ground when he speaks.

"Are you kidding me?" I look at the ground too. It's how we always talk on the field. This way, no one knows what we're talking about.

"Look, we don't want this to be a simple strikeout. Let him kick the ball. Come on, Tammy, it's thirteen against one. It's only fair."

John doesn't wait for my answer. He said his piece and expects it to be done.

I bounce the ball hard and don't bother to catch it when it flies up over my head.

Only fair. Hmph.

The kid was stupid enough to challenge the entire block, and now we have to be easy on him?

CHAPTER FOURTEEN

New Rules

JOHN TAKES HIS position behind home plate. I turn around to make sure the team is on their marks. I nod to second base, and Big Danny shoves the rest of a candy bar into his mouth. Billy Rattle is at first. And somehow Greg McGinty has pushed his way into playing third base. Benny Schuster, who's normally at third, is playing the outfield.

"Ready when you are, Tammy." Muscle Man is so cheerful that I want to smack him.

Instead, I do what John Marcos said. I pitch a long slow pitch, the kind that I do for the under-seven crowd.

Talk about a gift. This pitch barely crawls over home plate. Even a runt like Muscle Man could send it flying.

Good thing he's stiff, because if he was as relaxed as Billy Rattle or John Marcos, it would have gone clear across the railroad tracks and onto Sunrise Highway. Bad enough that it sails past Big Danny and into the outfield.

"Come on! Move it!" I shout to Matthew Donovan, who's closest to the ball. Or was that Michael?

The Donovan boys reach the ball at the same time and collide into each other.

Muscle Man touches first base and keeps running.

"Throw it here," Big Danny yells, but the twins are too busy slamming into each other to pay attention to the second baseman.

Michael kicks Matthew in the shins. Matthew hurls a few choice curse words back at him. Benny Schuster scoots between them but gets pushed out of the way by both of them before he gets his hands on the ball.

Muscle Man rounds second, and Big Danny's hands are still empty.

A few of the other boys scramble toward left field and end up getting pulled into the fight by Benny and the twins.

"Let's rumble!" shouts Tony Mogavero, as he dives on top of the heap. All I can see is a mound of arms and legs. It's hard to tell who's who.

Left field is turning into a free-for-all.

The ball pops up from the middle of the crowd, landing splat onto a place where no one's standing.

Conchetta Marchetta runs from right field, steps over a pile of boys, picks up the ball and throws it to third, where Muscle Man is heading.

It's gonna be close.

Greg McGinty reaches for the ball. Muscle Man reaches for the base.

"Safe," shouts John Marcos.

The only chance we have of tagging him out is if he tries for the home run. "Come on, stupid. Run for home." I wish it so hard that I must have said the words out loud, because Billy Rattle gives me an odd look. Muscle Man stays on third.

Greg throws the ball to me, and it lands, rock solid, at my stomach.

Billy Rattle scratches the top of his head. "What do we do now?" He waves John Marcos over. Greg McGinty, without being invited, joins the group.

"He's on third. How's he going to kick?" asks Billy Rattle.

"He should have thought of that before he challenged everyone. I think he should forfeit his man on third. Those are the rules." I bounce the ball a few times to sound official.

"I'm not exactly sure there are rules for a game like this one." Greg McGinty looks me square in the eye instead of down at the ground like he's supposed to when we're having a talk on the field.

"How about we put in a runner?" says John Marcos.

"What? We've never done that before," I say.

"You've never played one against thirteen," says Greg.

"Hey, Benny!" shouts John.

Before I can take a breath, Benny's standing next to all of us, towering over everyone, even Greg, who's two years older.

"We need you to take third," explains John.

In a leap and a bound, Benny's on third base, waiting to run.

I look back at my team. Huh. My team. My players. The group that's supposed to stand behind me.

No one says nothing.

"Anyone know the rules about a runner?" I shout to the outfield. "Is this really fair?" I wave my arms at the base.

There's not a peep from anyone.

Big Danny sways back and forth. "I don't feel so hot."

"That's because there's a runner on third," I shout back.

"Maybe you shouldn't have eaten all that candy," says MaryBeth from way out in right field.

"No, something is . . ." Big Danny turns a funny shade of green. And then he hurls his ice cream and candy bars all over second base.

"Oh, that's disgusting!" cries MaryBeth, and the game is called for the day.

CHAPTER FIFTEEN

Like Gold

THE NEXT DAY, I decide to call for Muscle Man, just in case he has any ideas of not showing up.

"Where are you going?" asks MaryBeth, her blonde hair tied up with ribbons that match her shorts. I look down and notice her shoes match too. Jeez.

"I figured I'd call for him, in case he gets lost," I say.

"I'm coming with you."

I walk up to Mrs. Kutchner's with MaryBeth three steps behind me.

As soon as I knock, Mrs. Kutchner answers the door, smiling.

"Where's Muscle M—" I hesitate. It seems I've forgotten his real name.

"Hi, Mrs. Kutchner." MaryBeth smiles.

"Hello, MaryBeth," says Mrs. Kutchner.

"I was wondering if Douglas would be able to play with us. We're playing kickball and we want to finish our game," says Miss-Matchy-Matchy-with-her-hair-ribbons-and-sandals.

"Douglas," Mrs. Kutchner calls up the stairs, "your friends are here for you."

I want to correct Mrs. Kutchner and explain to her that I am not his friend. Something about the way she looks at me makes me stop.

Muscle Man's wormy voice floats down from upstairs. "Tell them I'll be out in a minute, Grandma."

Mrs. Kutchner, MaryBeth, and I stare at each other. Each one of us has a make-believe smile on our face.

"You still making those lemon drop cookies, Mrs. Kutchner?" I ask.

Before I can even finish, MaryBeth has her pointy elbow lodged in my gut.

"What'd I do?" I whisper.

"Don't be rude," she scolds.

"I'm not. I'm just making conversation."

Mrs. Kutchner laughs. "It's been a bit hot outside, but as soon as the weather cools, I'll make a batch. Would you girls like some?"

"I wouldn't want to put you through that trouble," says MaryBeth.

"It's no trouble." Mrs. Kutchner smiles.

"Yeah, that would be great. I'd love a big bunch." I try to sound polite. "Please," I add.

MaryBeth's elbow is back in my gut.

"She said it's no trouble," I whisper.

Muscle Man comes bounding down the steps, not at all like a person who is about to be destroyed.

"Hi, MaryBeth. Hi, Tamara. How nice of you to come and get me."

"Yeah, real nice." I walk him straight over to where the other kids are waiting.

"Oh, Tammy, before I forget . . ." Muscle Man pulls a paper out of his back pocket. "I told you I'd come through for you."

"From Kebsie?" I ask.

Muscle Man hands me the note.

I hold the heavy crinkled-up paper in my hand. It even feels different than a plain old regular letter. Now I understand what Tim said. Letters from your best friend are like gold.

"Aren't you going to open it?" asks MaryBeth. The others gather around me.

What Kebsie writes to me is personal and sacred. And the last thing I want to do is share it with the crowd.

I shove the letter in my back pocket. "Nope. Let's play ball."

MaryBeth doesn't budge.

"I'm not opening it now," I say.

"That's not what I'm waiting for." She crosses her arms in front of her.

I move toward the Rattles' front lawn, where the others are taking their positions. MaryBeth refuses to follow. Instead she grabs Muscle Man and pulls him back so the two of them are standing arm-in-arm, staring at me.

"What now?" I ask.

MaryBeth rolls her eyes toward Muscle Man and mouths the words "Thank you." Muscle Man looks like he's waiting for it too.

I roll my eyes at both of them. "All he did was pass on a note," I explain.

If Miss Goody Goody ever wrote a note at school, she'd know that you really don't thank the person for passing it on. It's just what you did. There's no way I'm saying thank you to Muscle Man McGinty.

I'm so busy staring down MaryBeth Grabowsky that I almost miss the ball Big Danny throws my way. "Let's get this game started," he says, and I want to run to second base and throw my arms around him for getting me out of this jam.

I give the ball a snappy bounce and take my position on the field.

CHAPTER SIXTEEN

Not Feeling It

Its TIME TO strike this kid out. I don't care what Greg McGinty or even John Marcos says. Not one bit.

Benny Schuster's still on third as a substitute runner, and I'm not giving those long legs of his a chance to leap on home. Muscle Man isn't going to score a single run on my watch.

I roll three good hard balls. I make no bones about it.

John Marcos is trying to catch my eye. I avoid him, which is a hard thing to do since he's the one throwing me back the ball.

The only person I make eye contact with is Muscle Man McGinty. And all he can do is sigh every time my pitches fly past him.

In no time, Muscle Man McGinty is out, and it's our turn.

Billy Rattle is up first. His kick is respectable and should have been a solid double. But Muscle Man can't play outfield and second base at the same time, so Billy flies home.

Big Danny is next. That kid can send a ball clear off the block any time he wants to. And that's exactly what he does.

"That ball went so high that maybe your uncle Neil Armstrong will find it when he lands on the moon!" I shout as Big Danny rounds the bases.

John Marcos, Benny Schuster, and one of the Donovan twins all have home runs. Even Conchetta Marchetta makes it to third, and then Tony Mogavero brings her home.

Our strategy is simple really. All we have to do is kick it where Muscle Man isn't. Each kick sends Muscle Man scrambling to the other side of the field.

Each time we make it home, we high-five. Billy Rattle does a victory dance.

The score builds up fast. In no time at all, the score is Tamara and team 10, Muscle Man 0.

We're destroying this kid. He is toast. No, he is worse than that. He is burnt toast.

Surrounded by all these home runs and high fives, I can't help daydream about the moment when Muscle Man breaks down and tells us that he never should have challenged us. I imagine him exhausted, panting out his words, and confessing to us all that he's a wormy liar.

I'm ready for him. I remember every lie he's told, and I'm going to get him to admit to every single one. The Neil Armstrong Uncle lie. The Training for the Olympics lie. The James Bond Eyesight lie.

I'll make sure that after he's done confessing to us kids, he knocks on the door of every grown-up on Ramble Street. I wonder if Mr. Grabowsky will use the words *slippery slope* when Muscle Man tells him there was no Mr. Softee truck. Maybe Mr. Pizzarelli will find his Broadway show lie so repulsive that he'll take him down to the station house, just to scare him.

Oh, I'm sure there'll be tears. Maybe he'll even beg for forgiveness. I bet the other kids will stand with their mouths hanging open, and I will try my best not to tell them I told them so. They will feel foolish that they were so easily led. They will tell me that I am wise. And they will turn a cold, cold heart toward Muscle Man McGinty.

Oh, the joy. The joy.

I study Muscle Man, looking for a sign. An eye twitch. A quivering lip. A deep breath. So far, nothing. He's giving no signal that he's about to crack.

If he needs to go a few more rounds before he breaks down, then we can too.

I glance over at my teammates. Not a tired one in sight. We are ready to go the distance.

Muscle Man still wears his ear-to-ear grin. And I can't figure out why. This game is ours.

Janie Lee is up next.

MaryBeth straightens out Janie Lee's hair. "Now sweetie, all you have to do is kick the ball and run."

I take one look at MaryBeth Grabowsky and her little sister, and I think I figure out why Muscle Man is smiling.

We have a weak link.

"Maybe Janie Lee should sit this one out," I say.

"Are you kidding?" asks Big Danny.

"No way," says John Marcos. "The score is 10 to nothing, Tamara. What's the problem?"

The problem is that Janie Lee is only five. She's an easy out, even for Muscle Man. I count the kids on our team. If Janie Lee is out every time she's up, then the score could only be thirty-four to nothing before Muscle Man is up again.

Thirty-four to nothing. That's not enough.

"This game is too important," I say, ignoring the pouty look on Janie Lee's face.

MaryBeth puts her hand on Janie Lee's shoulder. "If my sister doesn't play, then I don't play."

I shrug. But the truth is that I want MaryBeth to play. I want her to be here when Muscle Man breaks down. I want her to see him fall.

"Come on, Tamara, let the little kid play," says Big Danny. He puts his hand on Janie Lee's other shoulder. "I don't play either if she doesn't play."

"Me either," says John Marcos.

Even the Donovan twins threaten to walk if Janie Lee doesn't play.

"Okay, okay. She's up now," I say, finally.

I give Muscle Man my most dangerous glare, one that I hope shows him that even though my team is clueless, I know his plan.

I hope, for Janie Lee's sake, that the strikeout is quick and painless.

"Whenever you're ready, J. Lee," shouts Muscle Man.

Janie Lee nods, and he throws her the first pitch.

It's not the fast, get-down-to-business pitch that I would have thrown. It's a slow, easy ball. A baby pitch. Even Muscle Man, who has no pitching technique at all, can do better.

Janie Lee kicks it, but instead of hitting the ball head-on, she nicks the top of it. The ball hardly goes five feet. Muscle Man is all over it. He's got the ball in his hands before Janie Lee can take three steps toward first base.

Even Janie Lee knows she's out. She snivels. For a moment, it looks like she's going to cry. And it's a sad fact that whenever a Grabowsky girl sheds a tear, every boy on Ramble Street scampers to her side.

"Run!" I shout.

"Go to first base, Janie Lee!" yells John Marcos.

"Try your best, sweetie," adds MaryBeth.

Janie Lee heads to first base, running as fast as her five-year-old legs can carry her.

Muscle Man races toward her, except instead of moving at top speed, he moves in an exaggerated slow motion.

"I'm coming at you," he says, but he hardly steps off the pitching mound.

It's all pretend, and everyone knows it except for Janie Lee.

The truth is that he can tag her out seven times if he tried and three times if he only half tried.

Janie Lee reaches first base. Still out of breath from her long run, she throws us all a big Grabowsky smile.

"Way to go, Janie Lee!" shouts Big Danny.

"You did it, honey!" screams MaryBeth.

Muscle Man runs to first base and high-fives Janie Lee, as if they're on the same team. The other kids jump up and down, like it's the winning run in the World Series.

Muscle Man and Janie Lee race toward the group with their hands up in the air. Big Danny, Benny Schuster, Conchetta Marchetta, Billy Rattle, Greg McGinty, and, of course, MaryBeth, all high-five them.

It's like one big love festival, and I'm the only one not feeling it. It's incredible. The kid doesn't even lose when he's losing.

CHAPTER SEVENTEEN

Kebsie's Letter

I CARRY KEBSIE's letter with me all day. After fifty days of missing her, it feels good to have her around, even if it's just in paper form.

Something inside me isn't in a hurry. So I keep her letter with me. And wait.

I wait until after everyone gets called home for dinner and the kickball game is done for the day. I wait until after Shirley fixes me a Swanson's TV dinner. I'm so busy thinking about the letter in my pocket that I hardly taste any of it, even the apple cobbler, which is my favorite part, even though Shirley never cooks it right and it always sticks to the aluminum tray. I wait until Marshall and

Shirley are sound asleep and the only things awake on Ramble Street are the crickets.

I slip out my window and onto the garage roof. All this time, I didn't know what I was waiting for. But as soon as I see it, I know instantly. I was waiting for the moon.

The moon is only a quarter slice, and there are a few clouds in the way. My flashlight batteries are wearing out, but one good bang sends a light beaming.

I open Kebsie's letter slowly and carefully.

> Dear Tamara,
>   Thanks for the charm. I am doing good. I will tell you where we are sometime soon. I am with my mother.
>   MaryBeth got another Barbie doll? That's neato. Tell MaryBeth congratulations.
>   From your bf,
>   Kebsie

I read it again and again before the words sink in.

"Tell MaryBeth congratulations?" "Neato?" That's not the Kebsie Grobser I know. *Tell MaryBeth that Barbie dolls are stupid. Tell MaryBeth to make sure she gets her dolls muddy. Tell MaryBeth to wipe that prissy look off her face.* Those are things that Kebsie would say in a letter.

I wonder if Kebsie's in trouble. Maybe she's trying to tell

me something. Maybe "neato" is a secret code word. Maybe she's really trying to say, *Help! I'm being abducted by evil Soviet spies who are forcing me to tell national secrets!* But something lumpy inside me knows this is wishful thinking. There are no signs of worry or trouble in this note, and Kebsie doesn't know any national secrets.

This is a letter from someone who's too busy to write because she is probably walking around her new neighborhood using the word *neato*.

All this time, I thought I was something special. I guess I was just someone to hang out with while Kebsie Grobser lived on Ramble Street. I was nothing to her.

There's no name for the feeling inside of me. The emptiness I got from missing Kebsie seems like good times compared to this new feeling.

I rip up the letter and promise myself that I'll never, ever write to her again.

CHAPTER EIGHTEEN

The War Comes Home to Ramble Street

THE NEXT DAY, my own team pulls a fast one on me.

We're lined up at home plate when MaryBeth Grabowsky drops a bombshell. "Janie Lee and I were talking about it last night. We think it would be a nice thing to give Muscle Man another chance to kick."

Janie Lee jumps up and down in agreement.

"I'd be okay with that," says John Marcos, and MaryBeth smiles.

"But it's our turn. We're up. He shouldn't be up until he earns it," I protest.

"The score is 43 to nothing. What harm would it do?" asks Big Danny.

Harm? What harm? It would change the rules of kickball. Rules that we live by and think are important. What if we changed other rules? The entire game would be different. What if, instead of running to first base, we ran to third? Or maybe it's ten strikes and you're out. Where does it end?

"This is wrong." I stare at the pitcher's mound, where Muscle Man is patiently waiting.

The team puts it to a vote. I am outvoted.

It looks like I'll have to strike Muscle Man out all over again.

John Marcos signals for me to pitch a slow ball.

I answer with my fastest pitch.

"Are you gonna call it?" I ask him. "What strike is this?"

John Marcos throws the ball back at me. "Call your own strikes."

And that's what I do. "Steee-rike one," I say in my best umpire's voice.

"Hold on a sec, Tammy. I'm not warmed up." Muscle Man drops to the ground and begins doing push-ups. He then moves into a weird combination of jumping jacks and deep knee bends.

Jeez. The kid thinks he's a junior version of Jack LaLanne.

"Whenever you're ready, Jack." I smirk.

Muscle Man kicks at the air a few times. Finally, he gives me a nod. And I throw the ball.

My next pitch is exactly the same as the first one.

Even though he's seen this pitch before, Muscle Man kicks way too soon. His foot sticks out in front of him, and he holds it there while the ball rolls over home plate.

I look at John Marcos to see if he's going to call this one. When he doesn't, I shout, "Steee-rike two."

John Marcos picks up the ball, slow and with one hand, and tosses it back in a lazy way. The ball stops midway between the pitcher's mound and home base.

Muscle Man himself has to run after it. "Your pitching is really good today, Tammy," he says as he tosses me the ball.

"Still think you can beat us all?" I ask, to remind my team exactly why we're doing this.

Muscle Man doesn't answer. He's too busy looking at something way in the outfield. Ready or not, I throw my next pitch.

He doesn't even try to kick. For a second, I think the moment I've been waiting for is finally here. "Do you give up?" I shout, but Muscle Man only stares past me. John Marcos stands alongside him, and the ball drifts over toward the Grabowsky's front lawn.

"What now?" I head for home plate and grab the ball myself. If I have to be pitcher and catcher too, this game will go on forever.

"Look, Tammy," whispers Muscle Man. He points to a man in uniform walking down the block.

"What's a soldier doing on Ramble Street?" asks John Marcos.

"Look at those medals on his chest," says Muscle Man.

Whoever he is, he looks pretty official.

The others join us at home base.

"What do you think he wants?" MaryBeth asks.

"Maybe he's a friend of Vinnie's." I brush her question off, anxious to get on with the game.

"If he is, I've never seen him," says Big Danny.

The soldier doesn't look like he's ever been here before. He checks each house number with a piece of paper he's holding.

He finally stops in front of the Pizzarelli house. He checks the number one last time. And then he marches to the door.

We all inch closer, waiting to see what happens next.

It takes a while for the door to open. Poor Mr. Pizzarelli probably worked the night shift and was in the middle of a nap. I wonder if he's going to yell about being woken up, the way he did the time when Kebsie and I made too much noise outside his bedroom window.

As soon as he sees the soldier, he lets him in, and the door slams closed behind them.

"There you go. He's a friend of Vinnie's. Now, can we get back to the game?" I ask.

But no one moves.

"Maybe he came to tell Mr. Pizzarelli that Vinnie's dead," says Big Danny.

We all stare at Mr. Pizzarelli's closed-up door.

"Things are fine. My brother got a letter from him a few days ago." And I suddenly remember that I never told Mr. Pizzarelli. A ball about the size of the one I'm holding forms in the pit of my stomach.

"That happened in my old neighborhood," says Muscle Man. "That's how they told Walter Martin's parents. When Mrs. Martin heard, she fell straight to the floor."

"Yeah, right," I say, but the other kids circle round him.

"Didn't stop crying for a week," he adds.

"I've heard of this happening," says John Marcos.

Across the street, the grown-ups are gathering too. Mrs. Murphy puts down her gardening hoe and stands next to Mrs. Kutchner. Mrs. Grabowsky runs across the street so fast that she almost loses her sandal.

Then, Mr. Grabowsky turns down the block, swinging his briefcase, like he does every night on his walk home from the train station. Normally on days when the Mets are playing, nothing stops Mr. Grabowsky from getting inside and watching the game, but as soon as the ladies stop him, he puts down his briefcase and joins them.

A few minutes later, Vinnie Pizzarelli's Aunt Carmella pulls up in her old Chrysler. Before anyone can ask her a question, she rushes into the house with her head down.

Even Mrs. Grabowksy, who can find out other people's business in less time than it takes for most people to put their socks and shoes on, can't get to her before the Pizzarelli's door closes.

"I've seen this before." Muscle Man's voice is flat. "This isn't good."

"Ah, come on, it's nothing," I say, but even I am starting to doubt my own words.

"I saw two guys get killed on the TV last night," says Billy Rattle.

"So? That was on TV. Those people were acting," I say. Sometimes Billy Rattle has gravel for brains.

"Duh, Tamara. It wasn't a TV show. It was in the news. They're always talking about Vietnam. They show it on the news all the time," says Billy Rattle.

"Don't your parents ever watch the news?" asks MaryBeth Grabowsky.

"Duh back," is what I want to say. Shirley only watches Jack LaLanne and soap operas, and Marshall thinks television rots a person's brain. I bet Tim watches. If Kebsie were in a war on television, I'd watch every night, searching for a glimpse of her.

I bounce the ball harder. It echoes on the sidewalk.

That ball, slamming onto the sidewalk, is the only sound on the block. Even Muscle Man keeps his big mouth shut.

We all stand, huddled together, waiting for the soldier to leave. The kids on one side of the street, the adults on the other. Everyone, quiet and waiting.

As the minutes pass, the groups grow bigger. Somehow the people of Ramble Street have a way of knowing when something serious is going on. Even my mother leaves her television set and finds her way to the swarm of grown-ups on the other side of the street.

Janie Lee is the first of the kids to break from our side. She heads over to where her parents stand. From the way Mr. Grabowsky shrugs his shoulders and pats her hand, it's clear that he has no answers. All we can do is wait.

As soon as Mr. Pizzarelli's door opens, there's no need to ask if the worst is true. Aunt Carmella's sobs hit the sidewalk.

Suddenly, it feels like all of the air has been taken away from Ramble Street. I gasp to take a single breath.

CHAPTER NINETEEN

Shink. Shink. Shink.

Dear Kebsie,

What do you mean congratulating Mary Beth Grabowsky for her Barbies and since when do you say "neato"? How come you didn't tell me anything important, like where you are or what's happening with you?

After your last letter, which was miserable, I promised I'd never write to you again. But something terrible happened. Vinnie Pizzarelli died in Vietnam.

We found out yesterday. They said that he died a hero. Vinnie saved the lives of three of his troop.

The funeral service is on Saturday and Tim is coming down from upstate this afternoon. When Marshall called him, Tim cried. Shirley spoke to him too and then passed the phone to me. I told Tim that I couldn't imagine losing a friend like that. I mean, you moved away, but at least you're not dead.

Everyone is going to the service tomorrow. Well, everyone except for Muscle Man McGinty, the kid who lives with Mrs. Kutchner now. I heard Mrs. Kutchner whisper to Mrs. Grabowsky that it was "too soon" to take him, whatever that means. If you lived here, you would be going, I just know it.

Remember the day that you and I snuck behind Vinnie's beat-up Oldsmobile and threw a water balloon at him while he was checking the oil? And boy, did he get us back with that hose. Remember how soaked we all were? It's all I can think about.

I thought you'd want to know even though you left here without so much as saying a peep.

Your bf,

Tamara

"Oh, jeez," says Marshall when he catches me watching the soaps on Friday afternoon. "Not you too."

I don't say anything. Neither does Shirley, who's right beside me.

Ever since morning, when Shirley patted the couch motioning for me to sit next to her, I've been watching her programs.

Every once in a while, she fills me in. "Amanda is really innocent of the murder. But Bob wants her to go to jail because he fell in love with Ruth when they were both stranded on an island in Tahiti. Of course, Ruth wants to marry Alex, but Alex needs to recover from his amnesia before he can marry anyone."

The stories are very complicated. Now I know why Shirley must pay such careful attention.

Marshall mumbles something about brain decay and is about to shuffle off to the den with his book when the front door opens.

A stranger steps into our living room. At least, that's what I first think when I see the man with long hair, a beard and mustache, ripped jeans, and a T-shirt that says, "Peace."

"Hey, Beanpole," the stranger says.

"Tim?" I hesitate. Who else besides Tim and Vinnie would call me that?

Shirley throws her arms around him. "Tim!" If she thinks there's something wrong with Tim's ripped jeans and long hair, I can't tell.

Marshall barely holds out his hand. "What happened to you?"

"Not now, Marshall," says Shirley.

Marshall's face grows puffy, like it's filled up with things he wants to say. But instead of talking, he stands alongside me, watching Tim and Shirley with their arms around each other.

I want to run to Tim. I want to tell him how sorry I am, but something's holding me back.

"Tim," I say softly. "Vinnie's letter. I . . . I . . ."

His face is so buried in Shirley's shoulder that I wonder if he hears me.

After a while, he lifts up his head. "What about Vinnie's letter?"

I try to explain. I want to tell him that I meant to tell Mr. Pizzarelli, but that I kept on forgetting. I want to tell him the truth, but no words come out.

The only sound in the room is voices from Shirley's soap operas. A commercial comes on, one that has a snappy jingle.

"It walks down stairs, without a care
And makes the happiest sound."

"Tamara, did you tell Mr. Pizzarelli about Vinnie's letter?" Tim asks, with a sinking voice. Tim never calls me Tamara, except on very special occasions.

I still don't speak.

"It's Slinky. It's Slinky. For fun, it's the best of the toys . . ."

"You told Mr. Pizzarelli, right?" Tim pushes Shirley away and is looking right at me.

On TV, the Slinkys are marching, two at a time, down a wooden plank.

Tim stares at me, waiting for an answer.

Shink. Shink. Shink. I don't care how loud the commercial is on the television or how much the Slinky inside of me is grumbling, I can't add to Tim's sadness.

I take a deep breath and say the words I hope will make Tim feel better. "I gave the message to Mr. Pizzarelli. I told him about Vinnie's letter."

Tim sighs. My stomach does a backflip.

Tim gives me a smile, weak, but at least it's something. "Thanks, Beanpole. I knew I could count on you."

The Slinkys on TV fade away, but I know from the way my stomach twists and turns that the Slinky inside me has a lot more to say.

CHAPTER TWENTY

Vinnie Pizza

AT THE CEMETERY, everyone has a story to tell about Vinnie Pizzarelli. Cousins, friends, aunts, uncles, neighbors. They all stand up and tell about their special times with Vinnie.

Tim tells about how he and Vinnie both lost their first tooth on the same day. And about how they liked the same girls in school. And how Vinnie was the one who convinced him to go to college.

Marshall twitches. I bet he thought that he was the one who talked Tim into going to school. All this time, it was Vinnie, whose grades were bad like mine.

When Vinnie's cousin, Joey, tells about how when they were both five, they took all the doorknobs off of every door in the house, the crowd laughs. Vinnie's Uncle Joey tosses back his head and chuckles.

"This is just wrong," I whisper to Shirley. "You can't laugh at a funeral."

Shirley, who is standing next to me, just says, "Shhh."

There are tons of things I learn about Vinnie. Some of them I wish I could ask Vinnie about. I thought I knew him, since he was my brother's best friend and all. But each person says something different.

They say he was a brave man. I never doubted for a second that Vinnie was brave. It's the "man" part that gets to me. My father is a man. Mr. Pizzarelli, who is staring down at a blade of grass, sobbing quietly, is a man. Vinnie wasn't a boy exactly, but a man? That sounds funny. That means that Tim is a man, too. I look at Tim, who is standing next to Marshall, in a new way.

They say that Vinnie thought of his Aunt Carmella as his second mom. Everyone knew that Vinnie's real mom died when Vinnie was seven. Aunt Carmella is Mr. Pizzarelli's sister. She came over every day to take care of Vinnie when he came home from school. Vinnie always called Aunt Carmella "the old lady." *I gotta go. The old lady cooked dinner, and she spits nails when I'm late.* "Can't do it, Tim. *The old lady will get mad.*" But in a card he made for her only last spring, he called "the old lady" the world's best mom.

I glance over at Aunt Carmella, who's standing with her arms locked around Mr. Pizzarelli. When Vinnie's cousin holds up the card, she buries her face in a tissue.

They say that he was a practical joker. Well, everyone knows that. They tell about the time that he wrapped every car on Ramble Street with toilet paper. He even wrapped his own car so no one would suspect. He sure had me fooled. I didn't think he did it.

They say that his favorite color was orange.

That he always said grace before he ate.

That he believed that the 1969 Mets were going to go the distance and win the World Series. Behind me I hear Mr. Grabowsky whisper, "Amen."

That his favorite toy as a baby was a stuffed teddy bear named Merlin.

That he'd never leave someone in the lurch.

When everyone's done telling stories, seven soldiers fire their rifles three times. With each sharp crack of the guns, I feel Vinnie slipping further and further away.

They fold the flag that's draped over his coffin and hand it to Mr. Pizzarelli.

"On behalf of a grateful nation," a soldier says.

Mr. Pizzarelli clutches the flag to his chest. Aunt Carmella collapses, and it takes three Pizzarelli cousins to hold her up. Tim and Shirley sink into each other, and Marshall has his arms around both of them. I stand apart from them, until Shirley pulls me toward her.

All of Ramble Street, except for Muscle Man McGinty, huddles together.

The laughter has stopped. There are only tears.

Except for me. I look around and notice I'm the only one not crying. All I can do is think about a book that Mrs. Webber read to us, the one where Tom Sawyer and Huck Finn show up at their own funeral. And I expect Vinnie to do it too. He's the kind of guy who'd pull a trick like that.

Even when they lower the coffin into the ground, I keep waiting for him to come back and say, "Hiya, Beanpole," and joke with Tim and call Aunt Carmella "the old lady" and tell us that it was all a terrible, horrible mistake.

CHAPTER TWENTY-ONE

One Single Word

ON SUNDAY MORNING, there's a note taped to my front door. I recognize the crinkled-up paper immediately.

I wait, like I did the last time, to read by moonlight. But at night, when I crawl out onto the garage roof, the moon that greets me is only a sliver. I struggle with my flashlight. After three sharp bangs on the tar paper, it works.

> *Dear Tammy,*
>
> *Sometimes people mean more than their words say. Sorry my note was short. I wanted to say I missed you in the last note, but I couldn't.*
>
> *I am very sorry to hear about Vinnie*

Pizzarelli and I wish I could have gone to the
funeral. I just couldn't.

And don't be too hard on Muscle Man.
Maybe he couldn't go either?

From your bf,

Kebsie

"Wanted to say I missed you in the last note but I couldn't?" "Don't be too hard on Muscle Man?" Another lame letter.

Kebsie Grobser is turning into one giant disappointment. I'm about to toss the letter over the rooftop when I see something written in pencil way down at the bottom.

It's faded, but I hold it up to the flashlight.

"Arroooo!"

As soon as I see the word, I am filled with hope.

Kebsie wrote, "Arroooo!"

A hundred million bits of happiness wash over me.

Kebsie Grobser, my fearless friend who howls like a lone wolf in the moonlight, is back.

I read her note over and over again. I try to find more of Kebsie in it. I wish she'd said something smart-alecky. Or made a comment about Muscle Man, like "Don't take any guff from the runt." But there's nothing. The only thing that I can really hold on to is that one "Arroooo!" The rest of it is a riddle.

CHAPTER TWENTY-TWO

Who Says You Can't Learn from Television

I SPEND THE whole next morning reading the letter over and over, and I still don't understand it. The funny thing is whenever I had something that needed to be figured out, I'd turn to Kebsie.

But now Kebsie is the one who needs to be figured out.

Kebsie is a straight shooter. The girl says what she means and means what she says. That stuff about meaning more than words has me stumped. She might be trying to tell me something, but for the life of me, I can't figure out what.

I run my hands over the note so many times that the words smudge together. No matter how much I try, I have no answers.

I need help. I am desperate.

I go through my options of people to ask. It's slim pickings. First I think about showing the note to Big Danny. He knew Kebsie, and he didn't roll his eyes when she came his way, the way most of the kids on the block did. But Big Danny is such a boy. Anytime I try to talk to him about something serious, he makes lame jokes and changes the subject.

There's always Tim. He understands these things, but he's hardly been around. He spends all his time at Mr. Pizzarelli's. Besides, he's not in a talking mood these days.

For a crazy second, I think about having a heart-to-heart with Miss Know-It-All Grabowsky.

Instead, I go to the living room, where Shirley is watching her programs.

On TV, there's a commercial. A group of ladies are in a grocery store squeezing toilet paper. I wait for it to be over before I speak. "Do you think that sometimes people mean more than they say?"

Shirley pats the couch next to her, but I don't want to watch. I want answers.

I ask again. "Do you think people tell you things in ways other than words?"

"That's a very difficult question, Tamara," she says. But before she gives me a decent answer, the show comes on, and Shirley is lost in her soaps. I edge toward the kitchen, figuring my time is better spent making a peanut butter sandwich.

"Look." She points at a tall, skinny man on the television. "Don't you remember from the other day? That's Brad. See how he's telling Emma that he loves her? What he really means is that he loves her, but he loves Anna more. It happens all the time, Tammy."

Brad is holding Emma close, and I can't see how she'd know that he loves someone else. "How can you tell?" I ask.

"It's not easy, but you can learn a lot from the TV." She motions again for me to sit next to her. "Watch and learn."

The next scene comes on. Emily tells Michael to go to Peru in search of his treasure. "Now, why do you think that Emily says she'll be fine, even though her heart is breaking?" Shirley asks.

Before I can finish my shrug, Shirley continues. "She's hiding her feelings. Emily doesn't want Michael to know how much she's hurting."

Another scene comes on, and a bunch of ladies are sitting in a hospital room, telling the one in the bed that no one will notice her injury, even though she is wrapped up like a mummy with bandages and gauze. "Why do you think they're telling her that?" asks Shirley.

"Because they're the stupidest group of ladies to walk the planet?" It's probably wrong, but it's my best guess.

Shirley presses her lips together. "No, they're not stupid. They're trying to spare the feelings of their friend."

"Oh." I sink back into the couch, wondering if that's why I told the lie to Tim about delivering Vinnie's message.

"Relationships are complicated, Tammy. Friendships. Family. And especially marriage . . ." Shirley's voice fades. "Marriage is very complex. You'll see. Just wait till you start dating."

"Great." I sigh. On TV, a blonde woman smiles right at us. "Do they ever send notes?"

"What?"

"These people." I wave at the television. "Do they ever send notes?"

Shirley nods. "Sometimes they do. Notes are very mysterious. They are always filled with clues about other things. Notes are very tricky."

The blonde woman is crying now, and Shirley is captivated. But I have one more question.

"What about real life?"

Shirley doesn't answer.

I stand in front of the TV, right in between my mother and the theme song to *As the World Turns*. "I want a real-life example. Tell me a time when people said things and they really meant more."

"It's the same in real life." She motions for me to get out of the way. "Come on, Tammy, I've been waiting all week to see this part."

"How? Tell me." I hold my ground.

Shirley puts her arms on my shoulders, and I wonder if she's going to push me aside. Instead, she pulls me toward her. "Remember when you were upset at Vinnie's funeral service? When the people laughed?"

I nod.

"I suppose," she says softly, "what they were saying with their laughter was that they loved Vinnie and they're going to miss him very much."

Neither one of us speaks.

I touch Shirley's arm. "Me too," I say, and my mother nods.

The blonde lady is smiling again, and Shirley pats the couch again for me to sit next to her. Instead, I head back upstairs and into my room.

CHAPTER TWENTY-THREE

When You Can't Stomach the Truth, Try Some Cheese Fondue

THAT EVENING, SHIRLEY serves dinner in our backyard. She puts a large cauldron in the center of the picnic table and lights the flame underneath it.

"It's cheese fondue," she explains. "I thought since Tim is heading back to school tomorrow, we'd have something fancy."

Swirls of barbeque smoke float in from the Grabowsky's house next door. I try to guess what they're cooking. There's a hint of sweetness that makes me think of chicken, but then the smoky aroma of char-grilled burgers fills up both our backyards.

"Who wants homemade potato salad?" I hear Mrs. Grabowsky say. She always sounds like she's singing when she talks about food.

I take one look at the charred flecks of burnt cheese simmering at our table, and it takes all my strength not to shout out, "Can you pass some over to the Simpson's, Mrs. Grabowsky?"

Shirley places a piece of stale bread on a long fork. "See, you each take a cube and dip it in the cheese."

"Is this sanitary?" grumbles Marshall. He's so busy shooting nasty looks at Tim's hair that you could have put a king's feast in front of him and he wouldn't have noticed.

I close my eyes and imagine the hamburgers on the Grabowsky's barbeque.

I listen for the sizzle.

Next door, Mr. Grabowsky must have said something funny, because Mrs. Grabowsky, MaryBeth, and Janie Lee laugh. All three Grabowsky girls sound exactly the same. Their high-pitched giggles float into our yard with the barbeque smoke.

It's easy to pay attention to the Grabowsky racket because in Simpsonland, there's not much conversation going on. Although it is just like Kebsie said, every single one of us is saying more than our words.

"Tim, please pass me the bread cubes," says Marshall, but I can tell from his glare that it's not all he wants to say.

What he really wants to say is "Tim, please pass me the bread cubes, *and when are you going to straighten yourself out and get a haircut?*"

Now I'm pretty sure the sweet, tangy smell wafting over from the Grabowsky's is grilled chicken. I bet that Mrs. Grabowsky made some of her famous honey barbeque sauce.

"Here," grunts Tim, and passes over the bowl, but what he really means is, "Here, *and when are you going to stop working for the man and pay attention to the war and all the bad stuff that's going on in the world?*"

"Thanks," says Marshall, but what he really wants to say is, "Thanks? *This is the thanks I get for having to get on the 7:11 train every morning and go into the city to make money so I can pay for your college tuition so you could grow your hair too long and tell me that I'm working for the man?*"

Hamburgers. It's not chicken. It's burgers. That's what they're eating next door. Smoky. Juicy. Burgers. And I bet they're filled with Mrs. Grabowsky's special homemade relish.

"The food is good, Mom," I say, but what I mean is, "*Shirley, can we have a barbeque instead of fondue, and can you please say something that will stop Marshall and Tim from fighting?*"

"Anyone want a meat cube?" asks Shirley, but what

she really means is, "Anyone want a meat cube *for the cheese fondue I slaved over, and I will not have either of you ruining this precious family time so you both better simmer down.*"

But from the look on Tim's and my father's faces, neither one has any intention of simmering down.

"My pitching is really good this year," I announce. "And we're right in the middle of a game with this new kid—"

Marshall interrupts. "Are you still playing that game all day? You could try reading."

"In the middle of the summer? While I could be playing kickball?" I shake my head. "I can't see it."

"You are as obsessed with kickball as your mother is with her soap operas." Marshall waves his hand in the direction of Shirley and me.

I put down my fork and chew on a stale bread cube, trying to figure if what my father said is true.

"All kids like kickball," says Tim. "She's not obsessed. It's nothing like Mom."

This time, Shirley puts down her fork and chews. For a while the entire Simpson family does nothing but chew.

"Anyone want seconds?" Mrs. Grabowsky sings in the next yard.

"I do," cry the other Grabowskys at the exact same time.

"Anyone want seconds?" asks Shirley in our yard.

"No, thank you," mumble all of us Simpsons at the exact same time.

"Are you sure, Tim?" Shirley sighs. "I made it special."

Tim glares at Marshall. "I'm not hungry," he says.

"You could eat a little more. Your mother worked real hard to cook this food," Marshall says, and what he means is, "Your mother worked real hard to cook this food and *even though it's filled with burnt specks and is probably unsanitary, you are being ungrateful by not eating the cheese fondue.*"

"I'm tired of this. I'm leaving," says Tim. And that *is* what he really means.

"Where are you going?" cries Shirley. "I made chocolate fondue for dessert."

"Let him go," says Marshall.

Marshall and Tim stare at each other one last time.

Tim gets up to leave. "See you later, Beanpole."

But I know that means he's not coming home for a long, long time.

CHAPTER TWENTY-FOUR

I Never Asked

IT'S FRIDAY BEFORE the kids on Ramble Street get together again. We stand in front of the Grabowsky's looking at each other, like we're not sure what to do.

Finally, Big Danny picks up the ball. "Wanna play?"

"Yeah, let's get on with this game," I say, and I give Muscle Man my best you'd-better-not-try-to-weasel-out-of-this stare.

"I'm ready when you are." He gives me the same look back.

I head toward the Rattles' front lawn, but no one follows.

"What?" I turn around to the crowd.

Billy Rattle is the first to speak. "We were talking before

you got here. We're bored. It's not fun anymore. Why don't we play regular teams instead?"

John Marcos nods. MaryBeth, who's standing right next to him, pumps her head up and down too.

"Cool," says Big Danny, and he bounces the ball like it's all settled.

Everyone agrees, and I suddenly notice that the group has dwindled. Tony Mogavero is back with his Catholic school friends. Conchetta Marchetta and her sisters are off playing at their pool. The Donovan twins are probably fighting with each other somewhere, and Benny Schuster is probably telling them to stop. Muscle Man's older brother, Greg, is who knows where. Even Janie Lee Grabowsky found some friends her own age.

Muscle Man shrugs. "Well, if you all give up," he says.

"Wait a second," I hold my hand up in the air. "You're not giving up? You don't admit that we beat you fair and square?"

"You didn't exactly beat me, Tammy, you gave up," he says. "Your team is the one that doesn't want to play."

"No!" I grab the ball from Big Danny, who stands there with his mouth hanging open because no one in the world would ever dare to take a ball from Big Danny. "Not until he gives up. We're not done with this game. Not until he admits he's a loser."

The other kids groan, except for MaryBeth Grabowsky, who crosses her arms in front of her and *humphs*.

"These are the rules! We don't stop playing until he admits defeat." I can't believe I have to explain it to them.

"Jeez, Tammy!" says John Marcos.

"Doesn't honor mean anything to you?" I point to Muscle Man. "He called us out! He said he could beat us all!"

"Sometimes you're a real pain in the . . ." Big Danny takes one look at MaryBeth Grabowsky and changes what he's going to say. "Butt."

Billy Rattle points down the block. "What's Mr. Pizza doing?" he whispers, as if Mr. Pizzarelli could hear him from three houses away.

"It looks like he's digging a hole," says Big Danny.

"Who cares?" I ask.

"Jeez, Tamara, the man lost his son," says Billy Rattle.

MaryBeth throws me a look that would make a lesser person pee in her pants. But I don't need a comment from Billy Rattle or a nasty look from Miss Never-Said-Something-Stupid-in-Her-Life Grabowsky to know it came out different than I meant it.

I didn't mean that I didn't care. I meant that he has every right to do whatever he wants to the front of his house. Of course, I cared. I knew Vinnie better than anyone here.

I slam down the ball, and it goes flying off toward Mr. Pizzarelli's.

"Let's go see if he needs help, " says Big Danny.

Before I can utter a word, they're all halfway down the block.

I turn to follow them and see Muscle Man slinking away. He's headed toward Mrs. Kutchner's garage, probably intending to hide out.

I march over to tell the other kids, "Hey, guess who didn't come? Mus—"

Something about the sight of Mr. Pizzarelli makes me stop in midsentence. Knee-deep in a hole, he looks old and weak and tired. His skin is shiny with sweat.

"You need any help, Mr. Pizzarelli?" asks Big Danny.

Mr. Pizzarelli doesn't answer. It's like he doesn't even notice that a whole group of kids is staring at him.

"What's he doing?" asks Billy Rattle.

Big Danny points to a sapling with its roots wrapped in a burlap bag. There's a hand-painted sign next to it that says, "In memory of Vincent Paul Pizzarelli, 1951–1969."

We form a circle around Mr. Pizzarelli, one that's so tight I wonder if he can breathe. He gives us all a quick nod. Then he goes back to digging.

There's a sharp poke in my back.

"Can you move, Tammy? I need to get in." I'd recognize the wormy voice anywhere.

I step aside, and Muscle Man, who's carrying a shovel, jumps into the hole.

He presses the shovel into the earth and digs.

Shink. Thwump. Shink. Thwump. Shink. Thwump. Muscle Man and Mr. Pizzarelli share the same steady rhythm, like they've been shoveling together for years.

Neither one says a word, and I wonder if Mr. Pizzarelli even knows that Muscle Man is there. But then Muscle Man hits a rock. As he teeters off balance, Mr. Pizzarelli grabs his arm. As soon as Muscle Man is steady on his feet, the two go back to their digging.

Just as I'm beginning to think it's a nice thing that Muscle Man is doing, he slides into another lie. "They planted a tree for my mom and dad when they died," he says. "It's on the corner where it happened."

Nothing stops this kid. Not even the death of Vinnie Pizzarelli.

I roll my eyes at MaryBeth who rolls her eyes back at me. "Didn't anyone tell you?" she whispers. "His parents died in a car crash."

"Yeah, right."

"Tammy, it's true. It was in all the papers."

There's something about the way Muscle Man grips on to his shovel that makes me wonder if this time, it's not a made-up story.

"Both?"

MaryBeth nods through one of her looks.

"How was I supposed to know?" I whisper back, and I regret asking it the moment I said it. Because if you ask MaryBeth Grabowsky a question, she always has an answer.

She folds her arms in front of her. "You could have talked to him. It's called having a conversation, Tamara."

"Duh. Why did you think he's in a foster home?" Billy Rattle chimes in, and his voice is hardly a whisper.

"I didn't know." The truth is I hadn't thought about it. Not even once.

I never asked Kebsie about her family, either. Not even once.

"When?" I ask.

"Three months ago," she says.

"Are you sure?"

"Jeez, Tamara. Didn't you notice he wasn't at Vinnie's funeral?" says Big Danny.

Of course, I noticed.

"Mrs. Kutchner was worried about him going to one so soon after his parents'," says MaryBeth.

If Muscle Man hears us talking, he sure doesn't let on. He's so busy digging that he's covered with sweat, like Mr. Pizzarelli.

"What kind of tree is it?" asks Muscle Man without skipping a *shink-thwump* of his shovel.

"A pear tree," says Mr. Pizzarelli.

"Mine too," says Muscle Man.

Mr. Pizzarelli holds on to Muscle Man, like he needs him for balance. Big Danny jumps in and helps steady him from the other side. Then, when it seems like Mr. Pizzarelli can stand on his own two feet, Big Danny begins digging out the dirt with his bare hands.

John Marcos pulls the burlap off the tree's roots. Everyone else is silent, watching. Billy Rattle's hand is placed over his heart, like he's about to say the pledge. MaryBeth has her hands clasped like she's praying.

Mr. Pizzarelli lifts the tree into the hole, and we all take turns putting dirt around the roots. "Do you want to say a prayer for Vinnie? That's what we did when we planted our tree," says Muscle Man.

Mr. Pizzarelli takes a deep breath, and it looks like he has to try a few times before his words come out. "That would be nice."

When we're done, Mr. Pizzarelli puts his arm on Muscle Man's shoulder. "Do you want to say a prayer for your mother and father?"

And that's what he does. When he finishes, every single one of us says, "Amen."

CHAPTER TWENTY-FIVE

The Last Note

THAT AFTERNOON, THERE'S another note taped on my front door.

I miss Kebsie so much I can't wait for the moon.

I run upstairs and open it quick.

Dear Tammy,

Sometimes people have to go without getting a chance to say good-bye. I'm sorry I had to. I hope we can still be friends.

You wanted me to tell you a story about my new life with my mom. I have a story about a

boy who lives nearby. He gave me seven hair
ribbons. I think I'll marry him one day.
  From your bf,
  Kebsie

I rip the letter into a thousand pieces and storm out onto Ramble Street.

It doesn't take me long before I see him, sitting in front of his house alone.

"Hiya, Tammy." Muscle Man is so busy smiling that he doesn't see the first punch. It's a good left hook. Vinnie Pizzarelli, who taught me how to fight, would have been proud.

"How could you do it?" I scream. "Why did you write them?"

Before he can open his big mouth, I pummel him again.

"How'd you know about the howls? About the 'Arroooo'?"

For this one, I'll wait three seconds. He answers in two.

"I heard you once, and I asked MaryBeth about it." His mouth is full of dirt, so his words come out muffled.

Big Danny and John Marcos fly in from nowhere. It takes both boys to pull me off of the kid. Vinnie would have been proud of that, too. MaryBeth runs from her house straight to Muscle Man.

"What's your problem, Tamara Ann Simpson?" she screams.

Muscle Man wipes blood from his face. "It's okay, MaryBeth. Tammy and I were just horsing around. Don't get mad at her."

"You phony!" I scream. "Why don't you tell them what you did?"

And the runt tells them everything.

"You faked letters from Kebsie Grobser? Why?" asks Big Danny.

Muscle Man is sobbing now. "Cause I didn't want Tammy to hurt anymore. Cause I wanted Kebsie to be the one who came back."

"I don't know what you're talking about, you wormy liar." I try to break free so I can give him one last punch, but Big Danny and John Marcos are holding me good.

"Think about it, Tammy," shouts MaryBeth.

MaryBeth helps Muscle Man into the house, and I know that as soon as Mrs. Kutchner sees the blood on Muscle Man's face, I'll be grounded for the rest of the summer.

CHAPTER TWENTY-SIX

Tang

SUNDAY MORNING, I open up my bedroom window and stick my head way out so I can get a good look at what's going on at the Grabowsky's. Even though it looks like it's going to rain, the family is buzzing around their yard, getting ready for the moon-walk party.

"Let's have hot dogs made into little rocket ships," says Mrs. Grabowsky. I'm sure she knows I'm watching, because her voice is loud. I bet she figures my ears are still ringing from all the yelling Marshall did when he got home from work last night and found out what I'd done. "And we can have Swedish meatballs made to look like meteors," she adds, and I'm certain she's talking loud again to rub it all in.

"And marshmallows for moon rocks," says Mr. Grabowsky.

"All my dolls can wear their space suits!" says Miss Thirteen Barbies.

Mrs. Grabowsky claps her hands. "Yes, the ones we finished sewing."

"And I'll wear the one you made me, Mommy." Janie Lee jumps up and down.

Mr. Grabowsky heads into the house and returns holding a large wedge of cheese. "Look, we can make a Swiss cheese carving of the moon."

When I pull myself back into my room, it's business as usual. Unless you count the fact that I'm grounded until school starts as news, there's nothing happening at all in the Simpson house.

I head downstairs and find Shirley leaning out of the kitchen window, her neck strained in the direction of the Grabowsky's backyard. I wonder if she's been watching too.

"So, are we gonna watch the moon walk?" I ask.

As soon as she hears my voice, she pulls herself back into the room. "No, I don't think so." Shirley lights a cigarette, and I move away from the smoke. "If we were invited to the moon-landing party, we would have watched."

"We're never invited," I tell her, in case she thinks we're not going because I punched out Muscle Man.

"We were invited last year to their Summer Olympics party." Shirley turns on the television. "And we're always invited to the Rattle's barbeques."

"Those are different. Those are whole-block parties where everyone is invited, not special parties. We're never invited to the special ones."

Shirley sits up straight, waiting for her programs to flick onto the screen. "If you didn't hit that boy . . ."

I want to tell her that we're not invited because she watches too many soap operas and doesn't trade recipes with the other moms and never gets her hair done.

Instead I say, "I have an idea." I stand in front of the TV, like I did before. "Let's have our own moon-landing party. We could get marshmallows and pretend they're moon rocks. It'll be fun."

Shirley stares through me, like I'm not even there. "Maybe *next* time."

"But next time isn't the first time."

Shirley pushes me aside, her eyes fixed on the television. "I said not today."

Marshall's answer is equally depressing.

"No matter how many men walk on the moon, how does it affect me? I still have to get up and take the 7:11 train to New York and work for Mr. Rendizzi at the Manhattan Plumbing Supply Company." He's sitting in his easy chair, wearing the slippers that Tim gave him last Christmas.

"But Dad, this is history."

"You should have thought of it before you punched out that kid. Grounded means no television, too." He buries his face in a book.

I run to the basement, hoping Tim will call. It's been days since I spoke to him, and he doesn't even know about the grounding. I tape the Jimi Hendrix poster up on the wall for the thousandth time. I dust off his pictures, throw myself in Grandma's old rocker, and chant "Tim telephone. Tim telephone. Timtelephone. Timtelephone."

The phone rings, and I creak my neck toward the upstairs floor.

"I know, I know," says Shirley, "I can't believe that Brad would do such a thing." Shirley is talking about her soap operas, so she must be talking to my aunt Maria. Tim would never talk soaps. I let her voice fade into the distance, and I work on my magic powers. "Tim telephone. Tim telephone. Tim telephone."

Ten minutes later it rings again, but it's the St. Rose of Lima church reminding Shirley to leave her old clothes outside in a bag for collection.

Day creeps toward night, and I creep out onto the garage roof to check on the Grabowskys.

They're gathered around a giant piece of cardboard and a dozen cans of paint.

"Do you really think that we can make a good replica

of the lunar excursion module, Daddy?" I hear MaryBeth ask her father.

Mr. Grabowsky laughs. "I think that our version of the LEM will do everything but fly."

I know it's risky, but I lean my head off the garage roof so I can listen to Mr. Grabowsky explain how the astronaut Michael Collins will orbit the moon in the *Apollo* spaceship while Neil Armstrong and Buzz Aldrin fly the lunar excursion module to make the first landing.

"Can we drink Tang?" asks MaryBeth.

"What's that?" asks Janie Lee.

"That's a powdery drink the astronauts take to space," says Mrs. Grabowsky. "I bought some this afternoon."

MaryBeth gives Janie Lee a hug. "Just think, we will drink the same thing as the astronauts."

Mr. Grabowsky holds up the cardboard LEM for them all to see. The others step back to admire their work. "This is an important night for history," he says. "One day, your children will want to know where you were the night that the first man walked on the moon."

"And we can tell them all about our party," says Janie Lee.

"And how we watched it all together," says MaryBeth.

And for the first time in my life, I wish I was a Grabowsky.

CHAPTER TWENTY-SEVEN

Almost Reached the Moon
by Myself

THAT NIGHT, I try to sleep, but there's too much noise coming from the party next door. Every time I nod off, a string of laughter from the Grabowsky house pokes at me.

I can't help thinking about Kebsie. I wonder if she's at a moon-landing party drinking Tang and eating Swedish meatballs that look like meteors too.

I lean out my window so I can get a good look at the house next door. Big Danny and his parents hurry up the Grabowsky's front steps. Big Danny's mom holds a covered casserole. The Rattles are next, and I'm not surprised. Mrs. Rattle and Mrs. Grabowsky are always together, trading recipes that would make Betty Crocker proud.

It's an important night for history, but if my children ask me where I was during the first moon walk, I'll have to tell them that I spent the night grounded in my bedroom, watching the neighbors file into the Grabowsky's party.

I think about sneaking downstairs to watch the moon walk on TV. But the television in the living room is so close to Marshall and Shirley's bedroom that I'm sure I'll get caught.

Instead, I flop on the bed and cover my head with the sheets while the laughter from the party next door fills up my room, making it feel stuffy and tight.

I climb out onto the garage roof. At least I can take a peek at the moon. At least it would be something to tell my children one day, that I saw the moon on the night of the first moon walk.

It's foggy, and the moon is hiding behind clouds.

"There you are, Tammy. I've been waiting for you." A voice right behind me makes me jump so high I almost reach the moon without any *Apollo* rockets to help me.

"Kebsie?" I turn around, and when I see Muscle Man and his stupid smile, I feel really dumb for saying Kebsie's name.

"How'd you get up here?" I demand.

He points to the garden trellis. "I c-climbed," he

stammers, and I wonder why he's not worried about getting another beating. "I wanted to see you."

"Well, I'm here and grounded. I bet you're happy about it."

"I didn't mean to make you angry. I tried to give the letter to my caseworker, but she didn't know where Kebsie was either. And I couldn't be the one to tell you." He kicks at a piece of ripped-up tar paper, and it flies to the ground. "I just wanted Kebsie to come back for you."

The fog draws closer. "Me too," I say, and I go back to my search for the moon. "I believed you because I wanted it to be true."

"I wanted it to be true, too." Muscle Man looks up at the sky. "How'd you figure it out?" he asks.

"The stupid story about the hair ribbons. Kebsie would soon as grow bald than put a ribbon in her hair. Where'd you come up with that?"

There's a long pause. "It's how my mother met my father. She told me that all the time."

A soft breeze touches the treetops but doesn't quite make it down to the garage roof. Something inside me shivers.

Muscle Man tugs at my arm. "Come on, Tammy. Let's go."

"I'm not going anywhere with you." I fold my arms in

front of me and wonder if I look like MaryBeth Grabowsky when she's being prissy.

Muscle Man turns to leave. "How come you have to be . . ." He sighs. "How come you have to be so tough? Why can't you give me a chance?"

A chance? A chance for what. A chance to ruin my life with his stupid smile and his over-the-top lies that the entire town of Massapequa Park lets him get away with? A chance to take the place of Kebsie? Is that what he wants a chance at?

"A chance to be your friend," he says, as if I asked him out loud.

The second he utters the word *friend*, an emptiness sinks inside me, causing my body to become so heavy that I bet I gain a hundred pounds. Tammy Simpson, seventy-nine-pound girl with one hundred pounds of emptiness.

Kebsie was my friend. No one else will ever come close. She's the one I wish was here right now. Muscle Man with his wormy looks and his stupid stories can never be anything like Kebsie Grobser.

Never.

Even if I tried really hard to be his friend and even if he tried really hard to be mine back, it could never be like it was with her. And knowing that fills me with an unbearable sadness.

Muscle Man is leaving. He's halfway down the trellis. "Are you coming?"

I turn to the moon for an answer.

And get nothing.

But the new round of laughter from the house next door is too much to take.

"I'm not going there." I point to the Grabowsky's.

"'Course not. I have somewhere else we can go."

I follow him down the garden trellis, and we make our way down Ramble Street. The street is empty now, but neither one of us says a word. Too many houses have lights on and windows open.

All we need is one well-meaning neighbor to come outside and wonder what two kids are doing walking down the street at night and our journey will be over. I'll be grounded until high school.

We turn down Clark Boulevard and find our way to Broadway. The streets are slick and shiny from the recent rain. We walk down to the part of town where a few bars line the street across from the railroad station. I'm not supposed to go here because Shirley calls it "seedy."

We stop at Canyon's Pub. On summer nights, the door is always open. Swirls of cigarette smoke pour out onto the street. The light from the television inside the pub flickers the way a lighthouse does during a storm.

Muscle Man squats low and creeps inside. I follow him, on my hands and knees, across the beer-soaked floor.

No one notices two kids crouched just inside the door. I bet we could have walked right in and maybe even taken a seat at the bar. Even the bartender is watching the grainy picture on the television hanging on the wall.

"That's the LEM," whispers Muscle Man.

"The lunar excursion module," I tell him, because the last thing I need is a lecture from Muscle Man McGinty.

On TV, the hatch opens up, and a man in a space suit climbs down the ladder. When he gets to the last rung, he jumps.

And with that, Neil Armstrong, commander of the *Apollo 11*, takes his first step on the moon.

CHAPTER TWENTY-EIGHT

One Small Step

"ON THIS JULY TWENTIETH, nineteen hundred and sixty-nine," says the announcer on TV, "Neil Armstrong becomes the first man to walk on the moon."

The crowd at Canyon's cheers. Outside, the town of Massapequa Park cheers. I bet the whole state of New York is cheering and the whole United States and maybe even the world.

"That's one small step for man, one giant leap for mankind," a voice crackles through the television.

"Did you hear that? The very first words!" says Muscle Man.

"I heard them." I try to shush him so I can pay attention to what's happening.

"I'm gonna do that someday. I'm gonna be an astronaut and walk on the moon," Muscle Man says. "I'm gonna be just like him."

He points to the man he once tried to tell me was his uncle. I think about reminding him of that and of the fact that NASA doesn't take runts. I am sure that somewhere before they were trained, those astronauts took an honesty test. But instead I stay glued to the television set.

"What about you, Tamara? Would you be an astronaut?"

I shrug.

Muscle Man won't shut up. "They said this couldn't be done. Things they say are impossible happen all the time."

Neil Armstrong takes another step, and it takes my breath away.

"Imagine, that this is happening right now. Right as we're watching it," I whisper.

"I believe in impossible things," announces Muscle Man McGinty.

"Good for you," I say.

"Mrs. Kutchner says that one day, all us kids might live on the moon."

"Mrs. Webber, my teacher, told us that too."

"Would you go?"

I'd never thought about it. "I'm more worried about when I'll get ungrounded."

"Come on, Tammy, stop being such a stick in the mud and dream a little. Would you go?"

"Dunno," I tell him. I think about living on the jagged surface of the moon. Then I think about the houses that look the same on Ramble Street. I try to decide which place I'd like best. "It's a hard choice."

"Not for me. I'm going," he says again. "I'm going to walk on the moon."

Two large feet step between us and the television set.

"What are you kids doing here?" says the man. I notice he's the guy who was standing behind the bar. "Where are your parents?"

I stammer, not knowing what to say. Since Muscle Man's such an expert at lies, I hope he's got a good one now.

For a compulsive liar, he is strangely quiet.

"Hey, Lenny, it's okay," says a voice from the darkness. "I know these kids. Let them stay. I'll watch them."

I can't see a thing since Lenny the bartender looms in front of me. But Muscle Man worms his way around Lenny. "Hey, Mr. Pizza! Thanks."

Mr. Pizzarelli steps out of the shadows.

"Keep them away from the bar," Lenny mumbles.

Mr. Pizzarelli motions for us to follow and then motions

for the waitress to bring us two Cokes. We all sit down, facing the television, in a wooden booth—one that seems as sticky as the floor.

Canyon's Pub and Grill grows quiet.

"What's happening now?" asks Muscle Man.

"Another man is going to step outside soon," says Mr. Pizzarelli.

"Buzz Aldrin," I add.

When it's Buzz Aldrin's turn, I hold my breath, waiting for his first words.

"Beautiful . . . beautiful," he says. And then he adds, "Magnificent desolation."

"Desolation. What does that mean?" I whisper.

"Emptiness," says Mr. Pizzarelli.

"Magnificent emptiness," I repeat under my breath.

"Look at them. Hundreds of thousands of miles away from the nearest human," says Muscle Man. "Alone on the moon, just the two of them."

I wonder if they're missing their family and friends. I wonder if that awful feeling of missing someone can follow a person all the way to the moon. "It must feel very far away," I say.

Muscle Man nods. "Away from everybody, away from people they love . . . I bet it's very lonely." And I realize he's not talking about the moon or Neil Armstrong or Buzz Aldrin. He's talking about himself.

"I bet it is, too," says Mr. Pizzarelli. And I know he's thinking of Vinnie.

I glance down at my Coke. "It's lonely here on Earth, too."

Muscle Man nods. Mr. Pizzarelli squeezes my arm.

Here we are, three of the loneliest souls on Ramble Street, sitting in Canyon's Pub watching the first men walk on the moon.

And knowing that we are all lonely together makes me feel not so lonely anymore.

For a moment, Kebsie leaving, Tim being gone, and MaryBeth Grabowsky's party become as blurry as the picture on the TV set. For a moment, sitting right here next to Mr. Pizza and Muscle Man is exactly where I want to be.

Shink. Shink. Shink. The Slinky inside me untightens a tiny bit to let me know what I'm thinking is true.

I close my eyes, trying to take in every detail of every moment. This is history. I want to remember everything. The astronauts' first steps. The pitted surface of the moon. How the American flag on the television looks just like the one on the wall of Canyon's Pub. The musty smell of the bar. The warm Coke on the table. Some day, I will tell my children all about it. I will tell anyone who asks me.

It's getting late, but the grainy images of men on the moon keep pouring into the pub. As much as I want to stay awake, my head feels as heavy as a twelve-pound bowling ball. Muscle Man has already dozed off. His head rests on Mr. Pizzarelli's shoulder.

"Come on, kids, it's time to go." Mr. Pizzarelli pays the waitress, and we head back home toward Ramble Street.

CHAPTER TWENTY-NINE

One Giant Leap

We walk outside along the sidewalk across from the railroad tracks. Even though it's late, there are a lot of cars on the road. They flash past us; their headlights cutting through the fog.

I'm grateful that Mr. Pizzarelli doesn't ask me questions like if my parents know I'm out. He doesn't ask Muscle Man either. We walk home in silence.

Muscle Man rubs his eyes, trying to shake out the sleep.

"Mr. Pizzarelli." I clear out the lumps in my throat before I can speak. "I never told you about Vinnie, about how he wrote to Tim and told him that things were quieting down."

"Tim told me about the letter when he was here." Mr. Pizzarelli doesn't look in my direction, and I don't blame him. I wonder if he'll ever look at me again.

We walk some more. Muscle Man is more awake and turning back into his gabby self. He points to the sky above. "Do you think they're up there?" he asks.

"They're up there," I say.

"Hey, Mr. Pizza, do you think they'll come back?" asks Muscle Man.

Mr. Pizzarelli sighs and looks up at the heavens.

"So many things could go wrong," says Muscle Man. "There could be an accident . . . a terrible one."

Mr. Pizzarelli doesn't answer. The only sound is the *slap, slap, slap* of our shoes on the wet pavement. After we've taken a few more steps, Mr. Pizzarelli puts his hands on our shoulders. "They'll come back," he says softly.

Clouds cover the sky, and I'm disappointed. The moon should be beaming. It should be a full moon, all swollen with pride. After all, tonight it's the center of attention of the entire world. The stars should be twinkling in celebration. Instead, the moon is being shy, hiding in the clouds. And there's not a star in sight.

Finally, the moon peeks out. We all stop to take a look. "That's a waxing crescent," I say. I thank Kebsie for teaching me the phases of the moon.

"Vinnie knew all the phases too," says Mr. Pizzarelli. "He wanted to be an astronaut when he was little."

A car buzzes by, racing too close to the curb. Mr. Pizzarelli grabs our hands and holds us tight, like we're precious butterflies about to fly away. And I know that Mr. Pizzarelli's forgiven me for not giving him that message.

"I'm gonna be an astronaut," Muscle Man says for the fifth time that night, "and I'm gonna do it for Vinnie."

I'm not sure, but I think that Mr. Pizzarelli might have, for one tiny fraction of a second, smiled at that.

We turn down Ramble Street. We pass Mrs. Murphy's house. The roses from her garden make the air heavy and sweet. I bet with all the rain we had, she'll wake up tomorrow morning and find some new ones in bloom.

Then we walk past the Rattle's house. The kickball waits on the front lawn.

The Grabowsky's house is shut up tight. The party must be over. Everyone is gone, and the house stands in perfect order, the way it always does. The streetlight casts a strange glow on the front lawn.

"Look." Muscle Man bends down and moves away the feathery blades of grass. Right in the middle of the Grabowsky carpet of green is a dandelion. He pulls it from the ground. With a sweeping gesture, he hands it to me, the way a grown man gives a lady a rose.

It's a tiny dandelion, nothing more than a golden bud. "Well, this little guy had a lot of nerve." I giggle. I really don't know why Mr. Grabowsky makes such a big fuss about them. Even though the leaves are raggy, they're not really a bad-looking flower.

Before I put it in my pocket, I notice that Muscle Man did not get the root. The dandelion will grow again.

When we get to my house, we stop.

"Do you want me to talk to your parents?" asks Mr. Pizzarelli.

I shake my head. "Nah, I'll talk to them in the morning. I'll explain what happened then."

I turn toward the house. Mr. Pizzarelli and Muscle Man stand there, like they're waiting for something.

Halfway up the walkway, I stop. "Thank you, Mr. Pizzarelli, for walking us home and for the Coke and for watching the moon walk with us."

"You're welcome, Tamara," says Mr. Pizzarelli.

I turn to the runt. "We got a game to finish."

Muscle Man nods. "We sure do."

But that's not really what I want to say. I walk a few more steps toward the door before I turn around again.

"Hey, Muscle Man." I take a deep breath and hope to high heaven that my head doesn't start to throb. "Thanks."

Muscle Man grins his stupid smile. "Anytime, Tammy."

There's one more thing I have to do before I face my grounding.

I wait until the moon shows itself one last time and lift my head up toward the sky.

"Arrooo!"